PUFFIN BOOKS

Editor: Kaye Webb

MR McFADDEN'S HALLOWE'EN

'It's fun being with Mr McFadden,' Selina told Ma and Pa, and they looked at one another with undisguised amazement. They didn't understand at all how satisfying it was for Selina, who always made such a mess of things at home, to go and help Mr McFadden at Drumlarach, where everything she did seemed to turn out so well.

She had not always enjoyed seeing him – in fact she had hated it when her stubborn pony Haggis kept bolting up the lane and into Mr McFadden's turnip field, and he the grumpiest, meanest, most frightening old farmer for miles around – but once she had bravely rescued him after his accident, and had got into the habit of visiting him because *someone* had to help the cross old stick when he couldn't walk, she found that he could really be quite nice.

Unfortunately, the more Selina grew to like him, the more the people in the village *dis*liked him. Soon they would not even sell him anything in the shops, and life was becoming very difficult – and even dangerous – for Selina and Mr McFadden before things started going right for them, and for the lonely little orphan Tim Scobie who was their friend.

Like all Rumer Godden's books, this is a story to remember. Also in Puffins are *The Diddakoi* (recently televised as *Kizzy*), and five books for younger readers, *Little Plum*, *Miss Happiness and Miss Flower*, *Candy Floss* and *Impunity Jane*, *The Story of Holly and Ivy*, and *The Dolls' House*.

Rumer Godden

MR McFADDEN'S
HALLOWE'EN

Illustrated by Ann Strugnell

PUFFIN BOOKS

Puffin Books, Penguin Books Ltd, Harmondsworth, Middlesex, England
Penguin Books, 625 Madison Avenue, New York, New York 10022, U.S.A.
Penguin Books Australia Ltd, Ringwood, Victoria, Australia
Penguin Books Canada Ltd, 2801 John Street, Markham, Ontario, Canada L3R 1B4
Penguin Books (N.Z.) Ltd, 182–190 Wairau Road, Auckland 10, New Zealand

First published by Macmillan London Ltd 1975
Published in Puffin Books 1977

Filmset in 'Monophoto' Baskerville
Printed in Great Britain by
Richard Clay (The Chaucer Press), Ltd, Bungay, Suffolk

To Charlotte
who was the good witch

The people in this book
live in the Scottish Border country
where the dialect is quite different
from the Highland dialect
with which most people
are more familiar.

'I shall be a good witch,' said Selina.

'A *good* witch?' asked Muffet. 'There's no such thing.'

'There will be when I am one,' said Selina.

In Scotland, where Muffet and Selina Russell lived, as autumn draws out, mysterious airs begin.

At first, autumn is quite ordinary; there are still late summer colours of heather and the rowan berries are scarlet; the light stays gold on the hills and the bracken is copper brown. There are days of heavy rain so that the sheep, with their horns and black faces, have their fleeces washed white, and the streams at this time of year run deep and dark brown, except when the sky is blue, when they glint reflected blue. Then, as the days get shorter, and the mornings, as well as the evenings, are twilit, colours fade, leaves fall and there is the smell of bonfires; as if as an echo of their smoke, mists begin to rise from the fields and swirl about the bouldered walls that are called dykes in Scotland. One of the first signs, to Selina, of the strangeness was when, all at once, innumerable little cobwebs appeared on grass and bushes.

'Who put them there?'

'Spiders, of course.'

'But why now? Why only now?' Selina thought them faery – not fairies with wings and wands, but touched with faery powers – special sort of spiders, but Selina, as Muffet often said, was the kind of person who believed in things.

Selina did not tell anyone, but this time of year always made her remember a poem their mother had once read to them; Selina could not say it all – Muffet recited much better than she did – but it began, '*Tis the witching hour of night*, and had a refrain:

> Listen, listen, listen, listen
> Glisten, glisten, glisten, glisten.

Then suddenly, at the end of October, almost every child in the village and the farms around, perhaps children all over Scotland, were on tiptoe with expectation.

Queer things began to happen in Menoock, as Muffet and Selina Russell's particular village was called; for instance, farmers were being asked for their largest turnips. There were secrets and whisperings and borrowings – often sewings as well. Hideously horrible masks appeared in Menoock's Post Office shop, but the best masks were made at home. Besides making masks, mothers and grandmothers, every housewife, were busy in their kitchens: they made toffee apples and 'tablet' which is a kind of fudge: squares of dark treacle tart: the grocer's shop ran out of nuts: apples were polished. In fact, it was almost Hallowe'en, the night when children dress up, and have the right to knock on anyone's door and be allowed in – only they have to pay with a song or a poem or a riddle. The people of the house guess who the children are – all of them are masked – and pay them in their turn by 'goodies', as Mrs Bridie called the sweet things and nuts. Mrs Bridie, whose house was next door to the Russells and who was more often in their house than her own, had lived in

Menoock all her life and no one knew more about Hallowe'en than Mrs Bridie.

'Ghouls and ghosties!' she told them and she chanted:

> 'This is the nicht o' Hallowe'en,
> When the witches can be seen.
> Some are black and some are green
> And some the colour of a turkey bean.'

'What is the colour of a turkey bean?' asked Muffet who would never accept anything until she knew all about it.

'I can guess it means a sort of runner bean, mauve-like,' said Mrs Bridie. 'You mauve your face all over. Mostly the bairns dress up in sheets as ghosts, but I have seen black cats and owls. My! I mind one year, there was a huge owl, and yin lad was a skeleton; his neep was cut into a head with marbles for eyen. There was Wee Willie Winkie – and yince I was a star.'

It was difficult to imagine Mrs Bridie as a star; she was more like a full moon with her big hips, big bosom, big face and high white hair but, 'It was gold, cut oot in cardboard round my neck. My! How it pricked. Why not be a star?' she asked the two girls.

'I'm going to be a bat,' said Muffet.

'I shall be a good witch.'

It should have been the other way round but then Muffet and Selina were, as Pa often said, topsy-turvy; they were even named wrongly. Muffet's real name was Margaret but she was always called Muffet – yet she would have made a good sedate Selina while Selina 'muffed everything', as Muffet pointed out. 'Oh Selina *dear*!' Ma would say while, 'Butter-fingers. Slowcoach!'

groaned Pa. Muffet called them, 'Mother and Father,' in a grown up way; Selina said, 'Ma and Pa,' and Ma and Pa needed a great deal of patience because Selina was often in trouble. Once, when their Great Aunt Emily had Selina and Muffet to stay and they were warned to be on their best behaviour, Selina took the biscuits thoughtfully provided in the guest room and stuck them together with chewing-gum. '*Disgusting!*' said Great Aunt Emily. She sent Selina supperless to bed and, in revenge, Selina made an 'aunt trap' for her on the stairs with strings stretched from side to side. 'Great Aunt Emily might have been killed!' said Ma.

Selina, too, was given to rages – 'And you all of eight years old!' said Mrs Bridie – and she made odd friends; for instance, Tim Scobie. 'A little lad that no one knows a thing aboot,' said Mrs Bridie. 'I wonder your Ma lets you, and him all dirty with a snotty nose.'

'Of course it's snotty. Tim hasn't any handkerchieves,' Selina told Mrs Bridie. 'I gave him mine but his aunt took it.'

'She'd take onything,' said Mrs Bridie. 'They're a disgrace to the village.'

Selina also had what Mrs Bridie said were 'notions', as for this Hallowe'en. 'It'll not suit you,' said Mrs Bridie about the good witch. Muffet, with her slimness, the graceful way she moved, her short dark curls and brown eyes 'that sparkled' as Selina said, would have made a fairy-tale good witch – 'If there is such a thing,' she said again – while, 'Selina is bats already,' teased Pa, but Selina still saw herself in a pointed hat, not black but rose-pink as Ma would make it for her, her apron snowily white instead of dirty and ragged, her petticoat and cloak pink too, and she would ride on a wand instead of a broomstick. 'You forget how heavy you are,' said Muffet.

Selina was heavy. 'A solid child,' said Ma. In the end-of-term display Muffet, who learned ballet and had just been put on her *pointes*, had danced a solo while Selina, among the nursery rhyme characters, was Little Jumping Joan – 'Little Thumping Stone,' teased Pa. 'I hate dancing anyway,' said Selina. She hated it, too, when people called her 'chubby'. 'Well, you are, you know,' said Muffet, but added, 'You have nice eyes. Not many people have eyes as blue as yours.' Muffet could be suddenly kind. Selina's hair, cut in a fringe across her forehead, was gold, which ought to have been all right, but it was usually so untidy that, 'It looks like a shock of corn,' said Ma in despair.

Nor was Selina an easy child. When her mind was made up, 'She's as obstinate as a kicking cuddie,' said Mrs Bridie. A cuddie was a donkey.

'No one has ever heard of a good witch,' said Muffet again.

'They will now,' said Selina. Then there was a crease in her forehead and suddenly she said, 'But Mr McFadden hates Hallowe'en.'

'Mr McFadden?' They all stared at her. 'What do you know about Mr McFadden?' asked Muffet.

Selina did not answer.

I

It had really begun the summer before, 'When we got our ponies – at last,' said Muffet.

Selina could hardly remember a time when she and Muffet had not had this 'pony-longing', as they called it. 'I'm afraid ponies are outside our compass,' Ma had warned them.

'Mrs Bridie says we can use her paddock,' Muffet argued, 'and her old shed.'

'But ponies have to be bought,' Ma pointed out. 'Pa doesn't earn enough for that.'

'Then we will,' and from that day onwards, a pig money box had stood on the table by the back door – a money box only for the ponies. 'Every penny of our pocket money must go in,' Muffet had said sternly. 'No sweets or anything else. Do you understand, Selina? You must never take a penny out. Swear,' and Selina swore.

Muffet had first put the china pig by the front door. 'Then visitors will see it and perhaps take pity on us and put something in,' but, 'Take it away *at once*,' said Ma. 'I won't have you begging.' But if either of the little girls were asked, 'What do you want for your birthday or Christmas?' they were allowed to say, 'Money towards our ponies, please,' and they were allowed to do tasks. 'I swept all the leaves up on the drives, our own and Mrs Bridie's, and my arms *ached*,' said Selina. They weeded and planted bulbs: in summer they picked fruit – strawberries, raspberries, blackcurrants and vegetables, beans and peas. They had even gone potato picking. 'Nowadays we think that's ower rough work for wee girls,' said the farmer who owned the potato fields, 'though my gran did it.'

'Let us try,' begged Muffet and, for the ten days of the holiday given in Scotland for what is called 'tattie howking', they toiled. 'And we got three pounds,' said Muffet; all the same, the china pig was terribly slow to fill. 'Two years,' Muffet had said that last July, 'and all we have is twenty pounds.'

'And eight pence,' said Selina.

'I think that's a very good effort,' said Ma.

'But it's not enough to pay for one leg of one pony.'

'I wish we could help,' said Ma. 'But there are so many needs . . .' The distress in her voice made Muffet say quickly, 'I don't really want a pony,' but Selina could not pretend like that. 'We do want them,' she said. 'But I don't think we're going to have them.' And then came the windfall; it had come as unexpectedly as an apple 'falling plop on the ground at your feet!' as she had said in wonder.

Pa opened a litter at breakfast, read it, stared at it and, 'Great Gordon's ghost!' said Pa in a low reverent voice.

'What is it?' Their three faces looked at him in consternation, Ma's, Muffet's, Selina's. 'What is it, Pa? What is it?'

'It's Great Aunt Emily.'

'Great Aunt Emily. But . . . she died last spring.'

'Good riddance,' muttered Selina and, the next moment, would have given worlds to have taken that back because, 'Yes, Great Aunt Emily. Bless her,' and Pa cleared his throat. 'She has left us each a hundred pounds.'

'Each?' They were dumbfounded. 'Not *each*?'

'Yes. You and me,' Pa looked at Ma, 'us and Muffet and Selina.'

'Not me,' said Selina. 'Oh, no! Not after the chuddy,' – she meant chewing gum – 'the chuddy and the aunt trap.'

'She says it's for all we did for her,' said Pa with a twinkle, but Selina was too upset to see it.

'But I did nothing, except bad things.'

'Perhaps Great Aunt Emily had a sense of humour.'

'And you did do good things,' put in Ma.

'I did her messages,' Selina said slowly. 'Messages' in Scotland are errands.

'Over and over again,' Ma was comforting.

'Well, she was a magnanimous and generous old lady,' said Pa and, 'Listen. Great Aunt Emily laid down that we were each to buy something we wanted and thought we couldn't have,' and, 'Ponies,' said Muffet and Selina with one voice.

Selina, as usual, had chosen the wrong pony though Pa had paid the same price for each and, 'I'm afraid,' said Muffet, 'it took some of his Great Aunt Emily money and Ma's as well because of the saddles and bridles and things.' Both ponies, too, were what Pa had said they must be: trained, quiet, safe in traffic and used to children. 'But there are children and children,' said Pa. Muffet's Dimple had turned out perfectly – Muffet rode really well now and had won two rosettes at the local show while Selina got nowhere on her Haggis. 'It's your own fault,' scolded Muffet. 'You would have him. Pa told you not to, but you would. You insisted.'

Selina had insisted but it was not for the pony's looks; Haggis was a thickset little pony, the dull colour of a haggis, halfway between dark brown and liver brown with an untidy dark mane and tail. Beside the sleek little chestnut Dimple, he looked still more shaggy and thick, 'Not thick, sturdy,' said Selina. She would not explain why she had begged for him but, long long ago – it must have been five or six years, because Haggis was eight now – one of the unknown children who had owned him had taught him a trick. 'Are you a good pony?' and Haggis was supposed to nod. 'Are you a bad pony?' and he should have shaken his head, but Haggis, 'being Haggis', said Muffet, had got it the wrong way round. 'Are you a good pony?' and he would shake his head. 'Are you a bad pony?' and he would nod. Selina could not bear it. 'He doesn't know why they are laughing at him. It's cruel of people to laugh,' and, though Pa and Ma and Muffet had all tried to dissuade her, she had begged so hard to have Haggis that they had given in. 'Which, I'm afraid, was a mistake,' said Pa because, besides teaching Haggis the wrong trick, some child had ruined his mouth, 'Tugging and pulling at the reins,' said Pa.

Selina tried to use her hands gently as Pa taught her, but that made not the slightest impression on Haggis. 'Use your legs,' said Pa. 'Put your heel in,' but Haggis's stout little sides might have been made of wood for all he felt.

'He's wood from head to hoof if you ask me,' said Muffet.

'He's not. He's glorious.'

'*Glorious!*'

'He is!' Nobody knew what Haggis could become

when he and Selina were alone: then she was Dick Turpin and he Black Bess, or he was the White Stallion, or a horse that danced in the circus, Selina his top-hatted rider, or he was the Queen's charger and she the Queen at the Trooping the Colour; he was even the horse with wings that only a poet can ride but, 'Look how he is at gates,' said Muffet which Selina had to admit was a justifiable remark. Where Haggis wanted to go he went and if Selina got off and tried, for instance, to lead him back to the gate, he would not stand still to let her shut it; he had, too, a habit of 'planting' as Pa called it, standing with his four feet planted, refusing to move and that was how Mr McFadden found him and Selina in his turnip field.

The village of Menoock was set in a glen so that, looking down from the high hills, it seemed a toy village. Most of the glen was farmland; fields with walls of grey boulders led up to the forestry reserves where, among the firs and larches, there were wide rides; to reach them, though, one had to go through the farms. 'I will speak to the Foresters,' Pa told Muffet and Selina, 'and get permission for you to ride your ponies in the forest, but you must ask the farmers to let you go through their land.'

'No one will mind if you keep to the edges of the fields and shut the gates,' said Ma.

Mr Gordon of Auchenbrae did not mind. 'Certainly, you can come,' he said to Muffet. 'Come whenever you like.'

Mr Douglas of Craigieburn was not as certain. 'Can I trust you to shut the gates?' 'We promise,' said Muffet.

'You'll be careful not to startle the sheep?'

'Aye, we'll be careful a'right.' The Russells were an English family, but Selina had picked up Menoock expressions, 'as if she were Scots born,' said Mrs Bridie.

'Well, we'll give it a try,' said Mr Douglas.

Mr Gordon of Auchenbrae and Mr Douglas of Craigieburn were kind – 'Quite kind,' said Selina – but then they had to go to Mr McFadden at Drumlarach.

Mr McFadden was the biggest landowner anywhere in the glen; his Drumlarach lay high on the hills opposite the Russells' house; often it was wrapped in mist and, so far from the village, so near the edge of the forest, it was somehow mysterious; the lane that led up to it from the village ran steeply for a good half-mile and there was no house near it. Drumlarach was apart but Mr McFadden owned the biggest fields, a fine Galloway suckler herd, a big flock of black-faced sheep – and the fields bordered the forest where there were 'delectable rides,' said Muffet, but, 'You'd better not go up there,' said Mrs Bridie.

It was not only that Mr McFadden was 'irascible', the word Mrs Bridie used, or that his sheep dog Lady was a good guard, 'There's also Big Wullie,' said Mrs Bridie.

'Who is Big Wullie?'

'A gander.'

'What's a gander?' asked Selina.

'A he-goose, you goose,' said Muffet.

This one, Big Wullie, was the terror of anyone who went to the farm. 'He took the seat oot of Jimmie Todd's breeks,' said Mrs Bridie. 'Not that I wouldnae like to do that myself.'

'I don't think I want to go to Mr McFadden's,' said Selina.

'We must try,' said Muffet.

Muffet and Selina rode up to Drumlarach. The gate
was open as was the gate from the farmyard to the turnip field that stretched down the hill below the house –
Mr McFadden relied on his dog and Big Wullie to keep
strangers out but now, though there was an angry
cackling, the gander, it seemed, was shut up. 'Well, I
were looking for the vet,' Mr McFadden explained
afterwards. 'He will no come if Big Wullie's aboot.'

'Please, we'll shut all the gates and keep to the
edges,' Muffet said to the big lean old man who appeared, blinking as if he did not like the sun. 'Shut
gates . . . keep to the edges. May we come?'

'Not on your life,' said Mr McFadden.

'We promise.'

'Bairns' promises!'

'We're not bairns,' Muffet said indignantly.

'Are ye no? I ken ye,' said Mr McFadden. 'Trmp-
ling yer ponies through m'steading, frighting the life
oot of m'sheep. Knocking stones off m'dykes. Dinnae
let me catch you at Drumlarach, that's a'.'

'Thrawn old devil,' said Selina as they rode despon-
dently home.

'Selina!' Muffet was shocked but Pa chuckled when
he heard. 'That's just what he is,' said Pa.

'He's like a horrible old tortoise,' said Muffet.

Mr McFadden was a familiar sight in the village
when he came down once a fortnight to do his shopping, always on alternate Fridays and he always
bought the same things: seven tins of stewed steak,
seven tins of corned beef – 'He eats everything out of
tins,' reported Mrs Bridie – tins of condensed milk, a

packet of tea, loaves of bread, a bag of dog meal, three bottles of whisky and a pound of Sobranie tobacco. He barely spoke, put down the money and carried the things away in a sack over his shoulder. He was a tall old man, 'Wi' powerful wrinkles,' said Mrs Bridie, such wrinkles that they made him look like a tortoise as Muffet had said. He wore an old tweed cap; his heavy boots were caked with mud though his trousers, jersey and worn jacket were immaculately clean and there was no dog in the district kept better than his Lady.

'Why do you call her Lady?' Selina, who talked to everyone, once asked Mr McFadden. 'Why Lady?'

'Because she's the yin female I ken who behaves like yin.' Mr McFadden's voice was so disagreeable that anyone else would not have spoken to him again, but Selina went on: 'How does she behave?'

'She minds her manners and does what I tell her. She doesnae blether.'

'She can't blether. She's dumb.'

'That's the yin thing that stops them. Clash-bags!' said Mr McFadden with venom.

Lady was not black and white as were most of the farm dogs. She was jet black all over, her coat shining like silk, and she kept close to Mr McFadden's heels. 'Well, it's good somebody likes him,' said Mrs Bridie.

'All the same, we don't want trouble,' said Pa. 'Now mind, you girls, keep well off his land.' That was easier said than done because it was just on Mr McFadden's land that Haggis wanted to go.

When Selina rode anywhere that brought her back through the village – 'and most of the best rides do,' she mourned – to reach Mrs Bridie's paddock where the ponies were kept, she had to ride past the foot of the lane that led up to Drumlarach and, every now and then, 'only it's getting oftener,' said Selina, Haggis would swerve and take off up the lane. 'It isn't "take off",' Selina had defended him. 'He doesn't go fast,' but it was such a determined trot that she could not dismount and had to sit in the saddle until at last Haggis charged through Drumlarach's open gate. It was then she met Big Wullie, a huge heavy bird with an enormous spread of white wings, a thick long darting neck, a fierce hissing and a wicked darting beak. At first Haggis was frightened and hastened back to the gate but there came a day when he took no notice of the fearsome gander, but splashed through the farmyard, scattering hens and Big Wullie's wives and, next moment, had plunged into the middle of Mr McFadden's turnip field. 'The very middle,' wailed Selina when she got home. He did it again, 'and again,' Selina said hopelessly. The hens would cluck, ducks quack, the goose-wives set up their cackling; Haggis did not care.

'Use your leg and your whip,' said Pa.

'I do. He takes no notice.'

'Then get off before the lane and lead Haggis home.' Selina tried but Haggis went up the lane just the same, dragging Selina with him.

The first once or twice Mr McFadden was mercifully out of the way; the third time he caught her. 'What the hell dae ye mean bringing yon rascal of a pony on to m'land?'

'I didn't,' gasped Selina. 'He brought me.'

'Well, fetch him oot before I do it for ye. He'll not like that, nor ye either. Take him oot, I say,' but Haggis had 'planted', and Mr McFadden, with Lady after him, had to wade through the turnips. 'Come along, wee man.' Mr McFadden's voice was different when he spoke to Haggis. 'Blaming it on ye, is she?' Selina guessed he would rather talk to animals than people. 'Come along,' and the amazing thing was that the moment Mr McFadden touched the rein, Haggis came meekly. 'So what were ye fretting aboot?' asked Mr McFadden. 'Noo be off with ye and dinnae let me catch a glimmer of ye here again,' but Haggis took Selina into the turnip field the very next day, 'And he doesn't even like turnips,' said Selina in despair.

'I'll be seeing yer Dad,' said Mr McFadden.

'Don't do that! Please don't do that,' begged Selina. She was nearly in tears. Mr McFadden's face seemed to wrinkle more and his eyes seemed to pierce deep into her as he looked at her.

'Are ye sae feart of him?'

'Of course not. He's just Pa.' Selina was surprised. 'It's not me – it's Haggis,' she explained.

'Do ye no' like haggis?' It was obvious that to Mr McFadden not to like haggis was unthinkable. 'It's fair tasty. Lady likes it, don't ye, old lady?' Lady wagged her tail.

'Not haggis to *eat*. My pony. His name is Haggis.'

'And it's haggis I'll make oot of him.' Mr McFadden went back to his wrath.

'Please don't say that.' Tears were in Selina's eyes now. 'Don't be like everybody else.'

'Everybody?'

'Yes. Pa told me not to have him. Everybody told me.'

'And ye would,' said Mr McFadden.

'Because it wasn't fair,' burst out Selina. 'Just

22

because he's ugly and awful and doesn't always understand, that's not his fault.'

'Everybody telt ye and ye went yer ain way.'

'Aye.' Selina sniffed.

'Seems to me,' said Mr McFadden, 'ye and I are much the same,' and for the first time his big gnarled hand patted Haggis's thick neck and, 'I don't think he's as horrible as they say,' Selina said to Haggis as they jogged home; but next time Haggis swerved and charged up the lane to Drumlarach she changed her mind.

That afternoon there was no sign of the old farmer, and Selina had to pull and coax Haggis out of the turnip field herself – it took what seemed to her an hour – and, when he finally came, it was at such a quick trot that she had to run to keep up with him; nor would he stop to let her get into the saddle. 'Haggis. Please. Good boy. Stand,' she panted, trying to get her breath. She did get one foot in the stirrup but he charged in at the yard gate almost brushing her off on the gate post. 'Hag-*gis*! I can't walk through the steading. Big Wullie's there,' she pleaded, and fought to hold Haggis back but into the farmyard he went and she had to go with him. Sure enough Big Wullie was standing by the pond. As soon as he saw her, he opened his wings, gave his gander cry and, with his neck outstretched, ran straight at her, hissing and flapping.

Selina tried to fend him off with her whip but, 'He wouldn't be fended,' she sobbed to Muffet afterwards. The farmyard was in an uproar; Big Wullie had set off the cock and hens and ducks; his three wives hissed as the great gander darted peck after peck. Haggis was pecked too. 'You deserve it. I don't,' Selina would have

23

said if she had had breath to speak. The pony pulled and plunged, jerking Selina's arms and knocking her riding hat over her eyes so that, as he trampled his way to the gate, she could not see and lost her footing. As Haggis trailed her in the mud Big Wullie gave her a peck behind. 'It's a wonder my jeans bottom wasn't torn out like Jimmie Todd's.' It was such a vicious jab that Selina gave a leap in the air. For a moment Haggis stopped; she pushed her hat up from her eyes and it was then that she saw Mr McFadden. He was standing by the gate laughing. *Laughing!*

'Please,' she called between gasps and sobs. 'Will you call Big Wullie off?'

'When I've a mind to,' said Mr McFadden.

'*Please.*'

Still laughing, and slowly, so slowly that Big Wullie got in two more pecks, Mr McFadden, in his huge boots, walked across the yard and, taking the gander by the neck, moved him out of the way. 'That'll teach baith of ye,' said Mr McFadden, and Selina's temper broke.

'I hate you,' she said. 'I hate you. I think you're the horriblest farmer in the world. I wish a tractor would run over you and grind you into dust,' and she swung herself up on Haggis, gave him such a hard kick and cut with her whip that he obeyed at once and, her cheeks red, her chin high, trotted out of the yard.

2

No one in Menoock could believe the news that broke
in the village that August but it was true. The Russells'
Great Aunt Emily, besides leaving her manifold rela-
tions, including the Russells, a hundred pounds each,
had left twenty thousand pounds to the village.
'Twenty thousand p . . .' Not even Mrs Bridie could get
further than that. She was too breathless with surprise.
'I do believe,' Mr McFadden said afterwards, 'that for
ten minutes not a Menoock woman spoke!'

The money was to be used for what Menoock had
always lacked, what Great Aunt Emily's will called 'a
recreation centre', but the villagers 'a Park'. There was
to be a flower garden with benches where the old
people could sit in the sun. 'When there is any sun,'
said Ma. There would be a bowling green, 'and a
ground for football and that,' said Mrs Bridie: every
day she had another tidbit of news. For the children a
playground would be grassed, 'with proper slides and
swings,' said Sellna; best of all would be a swimming
pool, 'and the water will be warmed!' said Mrs Bridie.

The Park was to be in the big field beside the
Menoock School. There was nowhere else it could be
because the field was the only flat space; the rest of the
valley was built over, except for the heather garden
and even it ran uphill. 'There is nae a place you could
put a pin in save yon field,' said Mrs Bridie.

'We shall be able to look at our Park out of the
school windows,' said Muffet. At the moment they

looked on the school's ugly asphalt playground with its iron railings on which Menoock children had climbed and swung for at least a hundred years. 'We shall look at grass and flowers.'

'And at the slides and the swings,' dreamed Selina.

'Mebbe. Mebbe not,' said Mrs Bridie. She was abrupt when she 'dropped in' that morning.

'But Mr Doherty gave it out in school.'

'Mebbe he did.'

'Why do you say "maybe"?' Muffet was sharper than Selina. 'We have the money.'

'We have the money,' said Mrs Bridie, 'but we have nae the field.'

'Why not?'

'Aye. Why not indeed!'

'But who ᷄ . . .' began Muffet when Ma interrupted. 'It's not certain yet, Mrs Bridie.'

'Is it no?' Mrs Bridie's voice was shrill. 'He says he'll not sell, the gurney-faced old scunner.'

'Who?' said both girls together but Ma said, 'I don't think we should talk about it until we really know.'

'Certainly not.' Mrs Bridie was offended and gathered her things to go. 'I am not yin for talking out of my turn,' which was hardly true.

There was another site for sale, but it was away up the glen and, 'What is the use of a centre if it isn't in the centre?' asked Ma and added, 'It isn't as if he made any use of that field.'

'I know.' Pa was on the Park Committee.

'You can't make a man sell his land if he won't,' said Ma and sighed.

'As a matter of fact we can,' said Pa. 'But I should hate to do it.'

'Then we're not going to have our playground and the swimming pool and the garden,' mourned Muffet.

'But who does the field belong to?' Selina asked Mrs Bridie.

'Ask yer Ma.' Mrs Bridie was still offended.

'But who?'

'Old Nick for all I care,' said Mrs Bridie.

Best of all Selina liked riding Haggis alone, but, 'I should rather you rode with Muffet,' said Ma.

'She rides with Elspeth.'

'You can go too.'

'I can't,' and Selina burst out, 'She calls Elspeth "Eleanora".' Why that made Selina furious she could not tell but perhaps it was because Elspeth, in her turn, called Muffet 'Marguerite', which made her seem as if she were not Muffet at all. 'Her name's *Margaret*,' said Selina in anguish. 'At least, it's really Muffet,' but they took no more notice of Selina than if she had been a fly.

'Hsst, Marguerite! I've something for your ear alone.'

'Better whisper, Eleanora,' and, 'They have secrets; they make me and Haggis stay behind,' Selina told Ma.

'Well, you can't keep a secret,' said Muffet, which was not fair as Selina could; she had told no one about her encounter with Big Wullie and Mr McFadden but, for two weeks after it, in spite of the secrets, she had ridden with Muffet and Elspeth and, when they came near the foot of the lane to Drumlarach, she pushed Haggis up between Dimple and Elspeth's pony, Dandy Dick, riding between them until they had passed the lane. Selina had even submitted to the shame of

Muffet's snatching the rein and leading Haggis but there was soon opposition from Muffet. 'I'm not going riding with anyone who has a rope wound round her middle.'

'It's not a rope. It's a lasso.'

'We're going riding, not playing.'

Selina could not see why she could not do both. She had once succeeded in lassoing a cow off Haggis, but the cow did not mind enough; it looked a little surprised but went on grazing. A bullock might be better, thought Selina.

'She thinks Haggis is a bronco,' said Elspeth.

'Silly baby.'

Why did Muffet, who was quite a good sister in private, become so sneering and nasty when she was with Elspeth? When she became Marguerite? Selina turned her head away so that they could not see the tears that so easily pricked her eyes.

'Hasn't she friends of her own who would ride with her?' asked Elspeth, but Selina's were not those kind of friends. They were Mrs Bridie, Daffie Kirkwhistle, the milkman, and old Coggan who mended the roads. 'Imagine them!' said Muffet and giggled. 'Or Tim Scobie,' said Muffet in scorn. 'Mother, do you know,' she told Ma, 'every day these holidays, Selina plays with Tim Scobie.'

'I don't think it will do him any harm,' said Ma.

'You know that's not what I meant.' Muffet was exasperated. 'I know,' said Ma, 'and I don't like what you did mean.' Ma looked serious. 'Muffet, if Tim comes to this house and you make him feel uncomfortable . . . well, I have warned you.'

Tim and his aunt had suddenly appeared in the vil-

lage. They lived with a man called Mr Evans in a caravan up the glen. 'Caravan! Pig sty,' said Mrs Bridie.
They were certainly not Scottish; in fact, nobody knew
where they came from, 'And nobody wants them,' declared Mrs Bridie – yet Selina obstinately wanted Tim.

He was a gnome of a boy, so undersized that he
looked five years old instead of the seven that he was.
'Well, his aunt gives him gin, that stops you growing,'
said Selina.

'Selina, you must not say things you don't *know*.'

'I do know. Mrs Bridie said so.' To Selina Mrs Bridie
was gospel.

Tim's cheeks were as pale as a Hallowe'en turnip, his
eyes deep sunken as though they were hollowed in his
small proud face; yet when he was interested, their
brown was bright, alert. His hair was seldom cut and
hung in dirty draggle-tails round his thin little neck. He
wore a man's flannel shirt with the sleeves rolled back,
and his pair of ragged trousers were held up by braces,
knotted to shorten them over his shoulders where his
shoulderblades stuck out like chicken's wings. His small
hands were hard and scaly – 'From housework if you
please,' said Mrs Bridie, 'poor mannikin,' – his nails
black-rimmed. Tim's gumboots had slits in them and
he never wore socks.

To have a pony was as far from Tim as to own a
private aeroplane, nor would he have said thank you
for one. 'A pony hasn't a steering-wheel,' he would
have said. His ambition was to have a bicycle, even an
old one. Tim indeed was 'different' and, 'I think you
must let Selina ride with you,' Ma told Muffet. 'She *is*
your sister.'

'Yes, worse luck,' said this cruel Muffet. 'But you

can't come,' she told Selina one afternoon at the end of the two weeks. 'Eleanora and I are riding up the glen to jump with Susan Poulteney Travers.'

'Susan would have me.'

'But we won't. Haggis can't jump. Anyway, this is for big girls.'

'I'll tell Ma you won't let me come.'

'Tell her then, you creeping clype.'

No one likes to be called a creeping clype – clype means sneak – especially when Muffet knew very well that in no circumstances would Selina have told Ma – and it was with a sore heart that she set out alone on Haggis. 'If you have ponies you must exercise them,' had been Pa's mandate and it had to be obeyed. She took her lasso with her and tried so hard to be a cowboy that she did not notice the direction Haggis took as they came out of the paddock. He turned up the village and, before Selina noticed, he was taking his determined way up to Drumlarach.

Big Wullie was in the farmyard with his wives and the hens and ducks, but there was no sign of Mr McFadden; nor did he come out of the house as Haggis plunged into the turnips and 'planted' there.

Selina became aware that there was a stillness at Drumlarach except for the cackling in the yard – and was not the cackling too loud? She remembered Big Wullie had not run at her though all the geese had crowded round her making their noises. Noises for what? It was as if they had not been fed.

She noticed, too, that no smoke was going up from the farmhouse chimney; in the next field the tractor stood deserted. Selina felt there was something eerie

32

about Drumlarach that afternoon; a pheasant, calling in the forest, made her jump and it was then she heard the wailing – a wail? A cry? Or a howl? A dog's howl. Haggis heard it too; he pricked his ears in a direction past the tractor to the Far Field. The howl came again as if a dog had lifted up its nose and was howling pitifully. Is it Lady? wondered Selina. Can it be Lady? There was no other dog at Drumlarach. It must be Lady – Lady howling pitifully. Perhaps she is caught in a trap; but Mr McFadden would set her free. There's trouble, thought Selina. I had better go and see, but Haggis was quicker. He was already hurrying through the turnips to the wall.

He would not go to the gate but scrambled over the low wall – Selina only just stayed in the saddle and several stones went tumbling; they made a noise and the howling stopped and there, on the wall of the Far Field, a black shape appeared. The shape was Lady and she showed quite plainly that Selina – and Haggis, of course – were doing what she wanted; she ran to meet them, circling round them, barking as if she were excited and relieved, ran a little way in front, looked back to see if they were following, came back to Selina and barked to urge her on. Haggis must have felt that too. 'For once he hurried his sticks,' Selina said afterwards; he cantered across the Big Field that led to the Far Field. Lady jumped up on the wall, still barking, but the wall of the Far Field was too high and Selina and Haggis had to go to the gate. Again, for once, Haggis stood while she opened it but Selina did not turn to shut it; as she came through into the Far Field her heart seemed to jump into her mouth; below Lady, close by the wall as if he had just climbed over it, lay

Mr McFadden on his back, his eyes open, looking at her.

For a moment Selina wanted to run away. 'Well, most little girls would have done,' said Pa, but 'Selina's doughty,' Mrs Bridie often said and Selina got off and, leading Haggis, she went up to Mr McFadden. At first she thought he was dead, his face was such a grey–white colour; then he spoke which made her jump. 'Och!' groaned Mr McFadden in disgust. 'When I heard the noise, I thocht it was someone.'

'It is someone,' said Selina. 'It's me.'

'What's the use of a bit lassie?' He turned away his head and even Selina could see the pain that he was in.

'I can get help. I'll go to your house and telephone.'

'Havenae got a telephone.'

'Why not?'

'Someone micht ring me.'

Selina did not point out that was the whole idea, nor that a telephone would have been useful now. Instead, 'What happened?' she said.

'Fell coming ower the dyke, fool that I was, and this bluidy great stane fell on me.' Selina saw that his foot was pinned under a jagged great rock.

'And it was you who told *us* we would knock stones out of your walls,' but Selina did not say it; Mr McFadden looked too ill and, 'When? When?' she could only falter.

'Last nicht, in t' dark.' Then he had lain there all night and all today! thought Selina.

'Dinnae seem to have the strength to move the damned thing.' He could not help a groan. 'Could easy were I on mae own twa feet, but it's the awfy pain.'

They seemed helpless and lonely there in the Far

34

Field with the forest looming close and the valley and the village down below the steep hill glen, far down and far away. There was no one but Haggis, Lady, Mr M'Fadden and Selina.

She bent and examined the big stone. She could not see Mr M'Fadden's foot at all, the stone hid it, but his leg was stiffly stretched. Though it was August, the smurr, or drizzling mist, was cold; she could see raindrops on the fir trees in the plantation near by, the grass was soaking and Mr M'Fadden's clothes were sodden. He groaned again and his face seemed to her even greyer. She wished she were one of those rescuing St Bernard dogs with a barrel of brandy round her neck; as it was, a feeling told her that it would be wise to get him quickly somewhere warm and dry but, 'Never move a person who has had an accident,' Pa had told her.

'What if it's in the middle of the road with cars coming by?' Selina had argued. 'Or if you were up a mountain in a fog?' The Far Field, though high, was not a mountain, nor the smurr a fog, but to go for help, particularly on Haggis, would take a long time; the nearest telephone, Selina calculated, was Major M'Bain's and his house was far up the lane, at least a half-mile, nor did she like to leave Mr M'Fadden. I must move him, thought Selina, and, 'Is your head hurt or your back?' she asked. Pa had told her that was dangerous.

'Why should they be? I told ye. It's only that I cannae move this awfy stane . . . off m'bluidy foot.' The words seemed to dwindle. Lady looked up into Selina's face and whined. Lady's eyes implored, 'Do something,' but the stone was too heavy for Selina to push, even though it would have rolled downhill. It was a queer jagged shape not smooth and round. Then Selina suddenly had an idea. She straightened up.

'What are ye gan tae do?' asked Mr McFadden.

'Roll the stone off your foot.'

'Dinnae be daft.' Selina did not answer; she was unwinding the lasso from her waist.

One end she put twice round the stone, pulling the rope taut. Her fingers were small to struggle with the thick rope but Selina was a Brownie and knew her knots. Mr McFadden watched and did not say a word, only set his lips not to wince when she touched the stone. When her knot was made, Selina took the loop end of the lasso and put it over Haggis's head and around his shoulders, letting the rope lie on his back. Then she turned him tail end to Mr McFadden. 'I see,' he said, pushing himself up on his elbow, then called, 'Mind now, the stane disnae fa' down on him.' That was a risk but Selina had to take it, a risk too that Haggis would 'plant' and refuse to move but Lady came to her help and began barking furiously at his heels. 'But Haggis had understood. I'm sure he had,' said Selina afterwards. He braced himself on all his four sturdy small feet and pulled.

Selina saw his shoulders strain but he pulled doggedly; the stone rocked, then came away with a jerk. 'God Almighty! Hell fire!' shouted Mr McFadden and fell back with a groan. Selina thought he was going to faint but he pulled himself up again. 'See . . . to . . . yer . . . pony.' The words came as if from far off but, as Selina was to learn, it was like Mr McFadden to think of an animal before himself, even when he was badly hurt. The stone had rolled clear of Haggis but when it came away the jerk had so startled him that he had tried to bolt, but was brought up short by the rope; now he stood sweating and trembling. 'Gan tae him. Clap him.' Mr McFadden said it though his own eyes were closed. 'He's gey brave.'

When Selina had soothed Haggis, patting his neck and talking to him, and loosed the rope from the stone, she led him, still lassoed, to Mr McFadden and they both looked at the crushed foot: Haggis bent down his neck and blew through his nostrils at the smell of blood, while Selina knelt and touched the foot gingerly; the thick welted gumboot was gashed and blood was beginning to well through the rubber; soon the boot was full of blood. Selina felt more than a little sick and had to steel herself not to whimper. How she wished Ma, or any grown person, were there, but I can't leave him here. He'll bleed to death, thought Selina, then – Haggis! Selina got up.

'Wha . . . t are ye up tae noo?' It was almost a whisper.

'That bleeding must stop. I'm taking you home.'

'Hame! I cannae walk.'

'I'm taking you home on Haggis. Look, I'll lead him to the wall. Can you get up?' asked Selina.

'I doot if I could.'

'You must.' In her anxiety Selina's voice was sharp. 'You must,' and as he did not move, though she did not know how she dared, she taunted, 'Cowardy, cowardy custard!'

A gleam came into Mr McFadden's sunken eyes. 'If I could get a hold of ye, I'd tak a stick tae ye,' but he got himself into a sitting position and edged himself nearer the wall.

'Can you?'

'Take t' saddle off,' said Mr McFadden.

Selina unsaddled Haggis and led him to the wall where Mr McFadden had inched himself up against it until he was almost upright. 'Be careful no more stones roll down on you,' said Selina.

'Aye.' It was a groan more than a word. 'Lead him . . . closer.' Again Haggis seemed to understand. He still had the lasso round his neck and, holding to that and the thick dark mane, Mr McFadden let himself fall

across the pony's back. 'Put your good leg over,' Selina
commanded and the long leg swung over Haggis's tail.
'Let the other hang down. Now try and sit up. Up!
Up!' Selina said it much as she spoke to Haggis and, still
holding to the lasso and the mane, Mr McFadden

managed to sit. His back was hunched, his feet almost touched the ground, but he was on Haggis's back.

'Come,' Selina coaxed Haggis. 'Come. Good boy,' and, walking unsteadily because of the heavy swinging burden on his back, the little pony stepped slowly down the hill.

'Leave t'bluidy gates,' said Mr McFadden. More than ever he was swaying from side to side. What shall I do if he falls off? thought Selina. I could never pick him up. The Big Field, when they reached it, seemed to stretch for miles and she was afraid Haggis would stumble over a mole hill; Lady kept the sheep off, making circles round Haggis, looking up at Selina for instructions, watching Mr McFadden with anxious eyes.

Selina was sure Haggis still understood. When at last they came to the gate into the Turnip Field he did not, as was his custom, brush against the post but, though Selina tried to lead him round the edge, he made his usual plunge into the turnips. It was nearly his undoing – and Mr McFadden's; the Far and Big Fields had been difficult going but here the ground had been ploughed and was soft and muddy. Haggis staggered as his hooves sank into it; he staggered another step, blew through his nostrils and stopped. 'Boy. Good boy. Come on . . . on,' Selina tried to encourage him; he took three uncertain steps, then gathered himself together and ploughed resolutely on. The turnip tops brushed Mr McFadden's boots which must have hurt his bad foot horribly but he made no sound; his eyes were shut and he was bent forward, his hands clenched, one on the rope, the other on a tuft of mane. As for Selina, she kept a tight hold on Mr McFadden's jacket and was trembling; what if he fell off on top of her, bringing Haggis with him? She could see the three of them thrashing about in the mud and turnips – but no, the little pony plodded through the sea of turnips until they came up to the farmhouse, white, thick-walled with its low slate roof. Lady ran straight in at the open door while the farmyard filled with a hungry clamour.

The door led into a kitchen, dark because of its little windows and cold because the door had been left open to the smurr and the fire was not lit. There was a dresser, a wooden kitchen table, a sofa covered in horsehair and a big armchair. He sits in that, thought Selina, but how, she wondered, could she get him from Haggis's back into it? Haggis knew; he walked straight into the kitchen – after all, it had a stone-flagged floor, not much different from the flags around the old-fashioned pump outside; fortunately, Mr McFadden was bent so low over the lasso and mane that his head did not strike the lintel; Selina led Haggis close beside the armchair and Mr McFadden tumbled into it. He lay back, his eyes closed, and again Selina thought he was going to faint. She remembered the St Bernard dog and, 'Have you any brandy?' she asked.

'Whisky . . . on dresser. I could do wi' a dram.'

An array of tins and bottles were on the dresser but Selina could not see any glasses or cups, nor any china. She found an enamel mug and two plates, one of which seemed to be Lady's as it held crumbs of biscuit. She poured the whisky into the mug. 'Tell me when to stop,' she asked Mr McFadden.

He did not seem able to tell her. Did the St Bernards give people the whole keg, she wondered? Yet a bottle seemed too much, even a mugful. She filled it half full.

But suppose I make him drunk? she thought tremulously, but 'I can guess Mr McFadden's insides are made of leather,' Pa said when she told him.

The whisky, though it made him less grey, seemed to have little other effect. Mr McFadden was shivering but Selina did not see how she could take off his wet clothes – in any case, she could not have got his trousers over the hurt foot in its boot and she knew better than to touch that. In the next room there was a big bed and she took a red quilt off it and a blanket and wrapped him round, putting a pillow behind his head. The shivers grew worse; she could hear the mug rattling against his teeth. A fire, thought Selina. I must light a fire.

There was a big old-fashioned black iron stove like the one in Mrs Bridie's house, with the same steel and blackened kettle standing on the hob; through the grated front Selina could see the fire was laid ready with paper, kindling and coal which was lucky but, will it burn, thought Selina? To make sure she put in a candle that lay on the dresser. She could not see any matches but, remembering that Mr McFadden smoked a pipe, she made herself dare to search in his pocket. He did not seem to feel her as she found them.

Kneeling, she lit the paper through the bars and watched while spirals of smoke went up; the candle caught and there were flames while the kindling started to crackle. Haggis snorted and backed but Mr McFadden, watchful even in his pain, put out a hand and caught him, holding his rein. When the fire was truly blazing, Selina lifted the iron lid and put on more lumps of coal from the hod which was mercifully full; she had to do it with her hands which made them black. Oh well! thought Selina, then, wiping her hands on her jeans, 'Now Haggis and I must go,' she said.

'Go?' For the first time Mr McFadden raised his head. 'Ye'll no gan away?'

'I must. I must go and fetch Doctor Dinwiddie.'

'Not on yer life,' shouted Mr McFadden, but all Selina said was, "Whisht.'

'I'll not stir,' said Mr McFadden.

'Then neither will I,' said Doctor Dinwiddie.

Selina had found Doctor Dinwiddie at his house and he had come at once. 'You had better go along home,' he had told her. 'I'll see to Mr McFadden.'

'I have to go back,' said Selina. 'I have to get my saddle and shut the gates.' After a moment she added, 'Please, Doctor Dinwiddie, don't tell anyone I found him. You see they laugh at me because Haggis – that's my pony – will go into Mr McFadden's turnip field.'

'It's a good thing for Mr McFadden he did,' and Doctor Dinwiddie said, 'I won't tell.'

When Selina had retrieved her saddle and carefully shut the gates, as she rode up to the house she heard such fierce argument that, half afraid, half drawn, she tied Haggis to the hitching post and went in. Mr McFadden was being his most disagreeable. 'Well, there it is,' said the doctor. 'I won't touch that foot until you come to the hospital and it is properly X-rayed.'

'What did ye do before ye had these new-fangled things?' Mr McFadden was furious. 'Ye used yer common sense.'

'I suggest you use yours,' said Doctor Dinwiddie. 'Come along, man,' and, as Mr McFadden did not move,

'Do you come or do I go? Choose.'

Slowly, reluctantly, Mr McFadden rose to his height and, with his arm round the doctor's shoulders, hopped to the door and stopped. 'What is yer name?' he asked Selina.

You don't know my name! That seemed incredible to Selina. Everyone in Menoock and the glen knew her. 'After all this time,' she could have said but, instead, 'I'm Selina Russell,' she said.

'Well, Selina Russell. There's corn in the bin under the dresser. I would be gratefy wud ye feed the fowls and geese and shut them up for the nicht.'

'Geese.' For the first time Selina quailed. 'Feed . . . feed Big Wullie?'

The gleam Selina had seen before came into Mr McFadden's eyes. 'Who's a cowardy custard noo?' he taunted.

'That's not fair,' said Doctor Dinwiddie.

'Whisht.' Mr McFadden was using all Selina's words – back at me, thought Selina. She tightened her lips but, when she went into the farmyard, the scoop in her hand shook so much she thought the grain would spill. The hens came running towards her, the ducks waddling after and Big Wullie, on whom she kept her eye, gathered his wives. She heard him cackle as he spread his wings. Selina almost ran but she felt something big, black, gentle and protective beside her. It was Lady. 'Would ye hu'd on twa minutes?' Mr McFadden had said to Doctor Dinwiddie. 'I'll jist send m' collie in to help the wee lass.'

With Lady in the farmyard Big Wullie behaved; he even stretched his neck out to Selina for some extra corn, just as he did with Mr McFadden and took it from her hand. Without protest he and the others went into their pens and, when Selina came back with the empty scoop and found the two men outside the door – they had been watching – 'Well done,' said Doctor Dinwiddie. Mr McFadden only whistled to Lady but, as he passed Haggis who was still tied to the post, he gave him a pat. 'Guid pony, are ye no?' he said and, wonder of wonders, Haggis nodded.

In the night the wind got up; when there were gales the wind blew up the glen and round Menoock's houses and down the chimneys as if it were someone wailing. It came into Selina's dream and she thought it was Lady's howling. Was Mr McFadden lost again? Selina tossed and turned and moaned herself. In her dream she saw his boot that grew bigger and bigger filled with blood; then the boot turned into Big Wullie who ran at her, his great wings open, his bill hissing. Selina half woke and found the hissing was rain. Was Mr McFadden still in the field? Had Doctor Dinwiddie really taken him away? Selina thought she was bending over the boot and suddenly she gave a piercing shriek.

The shriek brought Ma. 'Why Selina, wake up. You're dreaming,' and, as Selina clung to her, Ma soothed. 'It's only a dream.'

'It isn't! It wasn't!' and Selina began to shiver and sob as she had not sobbed on the hill.

Ma had scolded when she had come in late, but Selina had not said a word; indeed she had been so white and silent – and dirty – that Ma had looked at her several times. 'Are you sure you didn't fall off Haggis?' she had asked. Selina shook her head but Ma persisted. 'Did anything happen to you?' and Selina had been able to say truthfully, 'Nothing happened to me.' Now she sobbed it all out; Ma said nothing, only held her; then, 'We'll telephone Doctor Dinwiddie in the morning,' Ma promised, 'and find out if Mr McFadden is all right.'

'And you won't tell anyone?'

'Pa?' suggested Ma.

'Pa – not Muffet.'

'I think Muffet would be proud of you.'

'She w-wouldn't. She would s-say, "C-clever c-clogs".' Selina was still shattered by sobs. 'Why do I cry now, when I didn't then?' she asked Ma.

'I expect you were too busy,' said Ma, 'and now I'm going down to get you some hot milk and honey, and that will put you to sleep.'

'I wish Mr McFadden had some hot milk and honey,' said Selina as she sipped it.

'I expect the hospital will give him a hot drink,' but Mr McFadden was not in hospital. Selina found him next morning at Drumlarach, sitting in his armchair.

'I think I had better go up,' she had told Ma. 'Someone must let out the hens and geese and feed them,' but there would be no Lady and she added, faltering, 'I hope Big Wullie's not too horrible.'

'Take him some bread,' suggested Ma and it was while the gander was graciously eating it, 'out of my hand,' she told Ma, that she noticed the house door was open and smoke going up from the chimney; then Lady came running out as if to fetch her, and there was Mr McFadden.

'Ma said you would be in hospital.'

'Well, I'm no, aern' I?' His leg was up on a stool, the foot in plaster and he sounded in the worst of tempers.

'Wouldn't they keep you?' To Selina it seemed only too likely that no one would keep Mr McFadden.

'They wouldnae keep Lady,' he said which, to Selina, was a reasonable explanation: 'Of course he couldn't stay.' She was to hear all about it from Mrs Bridie; by now Mr McFadden's accident was common village knowledge. 'As soon as he came round from the anaesthetic – they had to set the foot mind; three bones were broken and it was crushed – if he didnae ask at yince for that dog. Doctor had left her in his car and offered to take her for the nicht, but the auld scunner wouldn't have it and discharged himself. God knows how he got hame. Come to that, God knows hoo the Doctor came to find him in the field.' Selina and Ma were silent. 'There's stubbornness for you,' said Mrs Bridie. 'The Doctor was upset but it stands tae reason, doesn't it, you cannae have a dog in a hospital?'

'I don't know,' said Ma. 'Hospitals are for people, not people for hospitals. He's an old man and never been separated from his dog.'

'And she would have lain quietly by the bed,' said Selina.

'Well, they wouldnae have it,' and, 'That matron!' Mr McFadden burst out now. 'Bossie mooth't bletherer!'

'I think I had better make you some tea,' said Selina. She did not like the look of Mr McFadden; his face was drawn and as grey as it had been in the field, his eyes half closed. She made up the fire and again brought a blanket and put it over him. He did not say 'thank you' then nor when she brought the tea, only, 'Is it strong?'

47

and added, 'I could hae made it mysel'. I lit the fire,'
he added defiantly.

'And it hurt you, didn't it?'

To her surprise he gave one of his unexpected
chuckles. 'The tractor didnae grind me into dust but
t'bluidy stane aboot did that tae m'foot.'

3

'There's no more tea,' Selina said next morning, 'and only half a tin of milk.' Mrs Bridie had been right: Mr McFadden seemed to have everything out of tins. 'And I can't see anything for Lady.'

'It's m'day for the village,' he said it slowly.

'And you can't go, can you?'

'Dang it!' Mr McFadden burst out again. 'Blast and dang it!'

'I'll do your messages for you,' said Selina.

'And blether it ower Menoock.'

'You know I don't blether. No one but Ma knows I found you. She won't blether either. If you give me a list, they'll think it's for her.'

'And I suppose yer mither smokes a pipe.' He said it witheringly.

'I have a Pa,' Selina reminded him. 'Well, choose,' she said, like Doctor Dinwiddie.

There was, of course, no choice but, when the list was made, 'Hoo dae ye think,' asked Mr McFadden, 'a peedie girl can carry a' that?'

'In my saddlebags on Haggis,' and, 'Mr McFadden gave me fifteen pounds! He trusted me,' Selina told Ma.

She had gone home before she went to the village, partly to get her saddlebags and partly to go through the list with Ma. 'What's Glenfiddich?' she whispered.

'Malt whisky,' Ma whispered back. 'Very good whisky. Three bottles. He must be feeling low.'

49

They whispered because Mrs Bridie was still there – and still talking about Mr McFadden. 'It serves him richt,' she was saying. 'Now he'll find oot where he is.'

'But neighbours will help him,' said Ma.

'No him, they'll no. He asked for it. Noo he can take the consequences.'

For Scots villagers not to help one of themselves in trouble was unheard of and Selina stared. 'I wouldnae make him as much as a cup of tea,' declared Mrs Bridie whose heart was usually gold.

'Why don't they like Mr McFadden?' Selina asked when Mrs Bridie had gone.

Ma opened her lips as if she were going to tell Selina something, then seemed to change her mind. 'Some people are not popular,' was all she said.

'Ye're a penny short,' said Mr McFadden when Selina had laid out on the kitchen table everything she had brought and had given him back the list and his change.

'I am not,' said Selina. 'I gave it to Tim Scobie for holding Haggis.'

'Ye – guid – a – penny – of – mine – to – that – boy?'

'Why should he do it else?'

Mr McFadden had no answer to that but continued to mutter under his breath.

'When you have been to the village, come back here,' Ma had told Selina. 'I think Mr McFadden needs something hot,' but, 'I dinnae want charity,' Mr McFadden scowled when Selina laid the dish on the table.

'It's not charity. It's Ma's pie,' but Selina thought she knew how Mr McFadden felt.

'What will Mrs Bridie say?' she had asked Ma.

'She can't say anything if she doesn't know,' said Ma. Now Selina could see Mr McFadden was looking longingly at the hot savoury-smelling pie. 'Ma made it,' she said, 'but I helped to make the crust.' He will take things from me, she guessed.

'A peedie thing like ye make crust like this?' said Mr McFadden with his mouth full. 'I dinnae believe it.'

'Do you not?' asked Selina. 'Then, just to show you, Ma'll help me to make you a bramble and apple tart tomorrow.'

'Ye're coming again then?'

'Well, you can't do without me, can you?' Selina did not say it, only, 'Aye, I'll be back this afternoon.'

'Maybe Lady and Big Wullie will be glad of ye,' was all Mr McFadden would say.

Pa came up with Selina that evening. 'Sorry to hear about this, Mr McFadden.' To any other neighbour Pa would have said 'McFadden' or called him by his name, 'Angus'. 'I thought perhaps someone should go the rounds for you.'

To Selina's surprise Mr McFadden scowled. 'It's no guid, Robert Russell, ye're coming seeking favour here. It'll no make a bit of difference and so I tell ye flat.'

Selina stared. How dared Mr McFadden speak to Pa like that? Pa said, 'I'm not thinking of you, Mr McFadden. I'm thinking of the beasts.' Selina knew nothing Pa could have said would more disarm Mr McFadden. 'You have calves and suckling cows and bullocks. They should be seen to.'

'They'll live.'

'Water?' asked Pa. 'I had better make sure it's running, and you hadn't started dipping, had you?'

All around, on every farm, farmers were dipping their sheep but, 'That can wait,' said Mr McFadden.

'Six months?' asked Pa. 'That's what Doctor Dinwiddie says it will be before you can really use that foot.'

'Doctors!' said Mr McFadden like a curse.

'He may be right,' said Pa. 'So perhaps you should let me get on with it. I'll see if I can get someone to help me this weekend.'

'Nae help,' growled Mr McFadden.

'The sheep have to be dipped,' said Pa, 'and I can't do it alone.' Mr McFadden grunted but did not contradict. 'Now I'll go the round,' said Pa. 'If I may, I'll borrow your tractor.' Silently Mr McFadden handed over the keys. 'I'll be back for Selina. She'll feed your poultry and get you some supper.'

'Humph!' was all Mr McFadden said.

Someone, probably Doctor Dinwiddie, had helped him to change his clothes; he was in clean trousers and shirt, an old red waistcoat and jacket, his foot still up on a stool. Selina opened a tin of steak – it was a struggle but she managed it. Mr McFadden did not offer to help her. She warmed the meat and gravy then brought Lady's biscuit and bowl as Mr McFadden curtly told her. 'Gie her half the steak.' Selina ladled it out and, 'I'll mix in the biscuit,' said Mr McFadden. 'She'll not take it from any yin but me.' Selina doubted that – Lady was pressing round her, looking up with glad eyes and wagging her tail – but she silently handed over the bowl. While Lady ate, she made tea and, with the rest of the steak and slices of bread –

there was no butter – she brought it on a tray to Mr McFadden. When he had finished and she had washed up the enamel plate and mug, she came and stood in front of him, her hands clasped together to give her courage.

'Yes?' asked Mr McFadden. His supper over, he was stuffing his pipe with tobacco. 'Yes?'

'I don't like the way you spoke to my Pa,' said Selina.

'Do ye no?'

'No, I do not.'

Mr McFadden lit his pipe with long slow puffs. 'Well, well,' said Mr McFadden. 'What are ye gan tae dae about it? Run away hame?'

'I'm going out to feed Big Wullie.' Selina turned away but there were tears in her eyes and Mr McFadden saw them.

'Look, Hen,' he said – Hen, which means 'my dear', is usually said to a grown woman and Mr McFadden did not say 'Hennie'. 'Look, Hen. Don't ye see how it goes against a body to have to thole all this . . . this . . .?' He looked at his foot, the tray of things Selina had washed up. 'This!' he laid down his pipe in disgust.

'And can't you see,' said Selina, 'that's how it has to be – for now?'

And that's how it was for the next two weeks, though Mr McFadden did not sit still in his chair for long. 'How he gets about on that foot I don't know,' Doctor Dinwiddie told Ma.

'It's incredible bravery,' said Ma.

'Incredible stupidity.' Doctor Dinwiddie was cross. 'I don't want any weight put on it yet, but he will.'

'It will set crooked,' he warned Mr McFadden. 'Do you want to be crooked the rest of your life?'

'That's what they say I am.' Mr McFadden said it grimly. He knew it meant 'cross and crabbed' and, swaying on his crutches, he tottered about the yard, though his face was ashen and Selina often saw sweat on his forehead. Pa came up every evening and went the rounds but he scarcely spoke to Mr McFadden and still no other farmer or neighbour came near – in the house there was only Selina.

'Man, you'll have to get a housekeeper,' Doctor Dinwiddie said on one of his visits.

'Thank ye. I have a housekeeper,' said Mr McFadden.

'Where is she?' Selina always hid when they heard the doctor come.

'I keep her in the broom cupboard,' which, at that moment, happened to be true, and Selina giggled.

'It's fun being with Mr McFadden,' she told Ma and Pa.

'Mr McFadden *fun*?' Ma and Pa looked at one another in amazement.

It was more than fun. Selina found a new satisfaction in looking after Mr McFadden.

At home she often bungled things, perhaps because everybody bossed her; at Drumlarach she was her own boss and everything seemed to turn out well.

'That Selina of yer's is a capable wee body,' Mr McFadden told Pa.

'Selina?' said Pa incredulously. 'Not Selina. You mean Muffet.'

'I dinna ken any Muffets. I mean Selina,' and, 'I always believed she could if she wanted to,' said Ma.

Of course Selina made mistakes – as the time when she washed Mr McFadden's pyjamas. 'Give me your dirty clothes. I'll wash them,' she had said.

'And how will ye do that with those peedie hands?' He would go on calling her 'peedie'. She was not all that little and Selina's voice was brusque as she answered, 'I'll do them in the washing machine, same as our own.' Mr McFadden did not like that. 'Yer mither won't want them in the hoose,' but Selina took them just the same. All would have gone well if, when she took them out of the washing machine, her eyes had not fallen on a large bowl of starch Ma had made ready to starch net for making Muffet's tutu. Muffet was dancing in another display and, 'She wants her name in the programme as Marguerite Russell!' said Selina in disgust. Starching, to Selina, was especially good washing and she put in Mr McFadden's handkerchiefs and, worse, his pyjamas. She could hardly fold the handkerchiefs and the more she ironed the pyjamas the stiffer they became and, 'I don't believe they're meant to look like that,' she told Mr McFadden.

'Well, they're spotless.'

'But can you get into them?'

Somehow Mr McFadden did and, 'He never said a word,' Selina told Ma.

'He's a nobler man than I am,' said Pa.

'How do you do your washing?' Selina asked Mr McFadden.

'Peg the clothes in the burn and let the burn wash them. Then put them in the sun or by the fire to dry.'

'Do you not have to iron them?'

'For why? They're clean. Am't I clean?' he asked belligerently.

'You are,' said Selina. 'But your house is beautifully dirty.'

'Dirty!' Mr McFadden sat up.

'Yes,' said Selina in ecstasy. 'You go in and out without taking your gumboots off – at home we have to leave them at the door. You don't have to wipe your feet – you can't, there isn't a door-mat – or keep your fingers off the paint, there isn't any paint.'

'I'm ashamed of ye,' said Mr McFadden. 'Ye coming from a guid home.'

'I know but . . .' and Selina went on, 'in a good home they're always cleaning and washing and ironing and washing up – Muffet and I have to do that. You only have one mug, just the two plates, yours and Lady's, and put things on them straight from the tin or the saucepan and eat them with a knife and bread – no forks or spoons or silver to clean. Look how you don't cook,' said Selina. She had quickly learned there was no need to fuss Mr McFadden with pies and soup; Mr McFadden lived mostly on bread and cheese and whisky. For his breakfast he made tea by the simple means of putting tea-leaves in the kettle which was dark brown inside. On alternate evenings he opened a tin of stewed steak or a tin of corned beef, half for him and half for Lady; the only difference was that he had bread, Lady had biscuit or the maize on which all the farmers fed their collies, 'and most dinnae get any meat at all,' he told Lady. 'Ye're pampered.' Lady wagged her tail and looked at him with adoring eyes.

'And *how* sensible,' said Selina admiringly, 'to eat on a newspaper instead of fussy table mats. You don't sweep the floor . . .'

'I do,' said Mr McFadden.

'You can't; there are too many things on it.' There were: kindling, a drum of paraffin, boots, bins of grain, while Mr McFadden's crook stood behind the door. 'You don't have to bother about spilling on the carpet. There isn't any carpet.' There was only an old sheep-skin as a hearth-rug. 'And I don't believe there is a duster in all Drumlarach.'

'It seems I have fallen into bad ways.' Mr McFadden sat staring at the fire.

'Have I ... upset you in your feelings, Mr McFadden?' she asked at last.

'How could ye – a no-nothing like ye? It's just ... Drumlarach was a braw bit place – yince.'

'It's still bonny.'

He shook his head. Then his most tortoise look came on his face. 'What the hell does it matter?' he said. 'There's only me.'

'Mr McFadden, would you let me bring Tim Scobie up with me?' and, as Mr McFadden looked forbidding, Selina pointed out, 'I had him before you. He misses me.'

'Think a lot of yersel', don't ye?'

'No,' said Selina. Candidly she did not. 'Why, even at school I was the dud. Now there's someone dudderer than I am. That's Tim.'

On his first day at school, Tim had done nothing but laugh until at last Mrs Riddick, his teacher, had said, 'You can't laugh here.'

'But it's here I want to laugh,' said Tim.

'It's nervousness,' said Mr Doherty, the head-master. No one knew what to make of Tim, not even kind Mr Doherty. Tim sat at the back of the class and refused to join in; when he was not laughing, his eyes filled with tears and he looked longingly out of the window as if he wanted to escape. Sometimes he had bruises on his face and if the teacher came near him, he dodged. 'Tim, does your aunt ever hit you?'

'No,' said Tim.

'Or your uncle?' Tim called Mr Evans 'uncle'. 'Does he?'

'Never,' but a big bruise showed at the back of Tim's neck where his shirt collar was too big.

Selina had seen Tim's aunt, a big slatternly woman, but only in the distance; she seldom came to the village – 'except to the pub,' said Mrs Bridie – and Tim did not like Selina to come to the caravan; they met in the village or by the river or Tim came to the Russells' house. 'She doesn't give him proper clothes,' Selina told Mr McFadden. 'He has to sleep on the floor and I don't think he has enough food.'

'Bring him,' said Mr McFadden.

Oddly enough it was Tim who made them clean up Drumlarach. 'If the windows was clean,' he said, 'the rooms wouldn't be half so dark,' and, mounted on stools, he and Selina tried to clean them, but they could not reach the top edges and, 'Och! they're all smears,' said Selina. 'If only we had Ma.'

'Mither? We don't want any mithers here,' said Mr McFadden and hobbled to the window. 'Here, get off that stool and gie me that rag. I'll clean them.'

'Go to it then,' said Tim.

The kindling went into the shed, the grain bins into the barn – Pa carried them – the gumboots were set in rows, coats hung on hooks and, for the whole of one afternoon, Selina and Tim scrubbed the floors; Selina soon ached but Tim kept steadily on. He was a surprisingly good cleaner for such a little boy – his aunt hired him out to earn a few pennies, scrubbing old people's

floors and house-steps on Saturdays and Sundays. 'At his age!' Mrs Bridie's voice was shrill with indignation. 'And him barely by being a baby. Well, I suppose wee yins used to work down coal-mines,' she said.

'I don't mind,' said Tim. 'I'm let into *houses*.' What Mrs Bridie, even Selina and Mr McFadden, did not understand was that, to Tim, people who lived in houses and people who lived in caravans were worlds and worlds apart.

His aunt's caravan was on a piece of waste land covered in rusty car bodies, tyres, old refrigerators and cookers, old sacks and trash, 'and mud!' said Tim, so that Selina's quite ordinary house seemed to him a palace; in his ragged clothes Tim hardly dared sit on the chairs. Drumlarach, though he loved the space, the high hill, the sturdiness of the house, could never, to Tim, compare with the Russells', so white-painted and orderly, 'But Drumlarach can be seemly,' said Tim and went to work. His muscles might be small but they seemed made of iron and he kept on scrubbing till the flags were clean. 'I'm only letting ye do this because I cannae catch ye,' growled Mr McFadden and Tim lifted his face and gave him one of his rare smiles.

'If a laddie works like that he ought to be fed,' said Mr McFadden slowly to Selina. He was not used to concerning himself with other people. 'I tell ye what. Hen, would ye go to the village on Haggis and buy a mite bacon and some tattie scones? I mind I used to like those.'

'Tim *will* be pleased.' Selina's face lit up. 'I'll ask Ma to lend us her frying-pan.'

'That ye won't. We'll buy our ain pan. I'll not lend nor be lent to.'

Besides the floor Tim scrubbed the kitchen table. 'Pesty little busybody,' said Mr McFadden yet he himself polished the oak dresser and blackleaded the big stove. 'Noo will ye whisht?' he asked Tim. 'Have ye done?'

'Almost,' said Tim, 'but I'd like fine for you to have

a new cover on your chair and a proper hearth-rug. And flowers on the window-sill. I'd like that.'

'Fallalls!' said Mr McFadden.

'Not fallalls; flowers,' Tim said firmly. 'Flowers growing in pots, so I could water them. Grown on purpose,' said Tim. He meant not wild flowers or weeds. 'On purpose,' said Tim, his eyes shining.

'You ought to have a telephone,' Doctor Dinwiddie told Mr McFadden.

'Humph!' said Mr McFadden.

'Hasn't this been a lesson to you? Suppose you fell with that foot. You wouldn't be able to help yourself.'

'Humph!'

'Suppose Galloway Blue Girl calved in the night,' said Pa. That was more telling and, 'They're no such fools,' Mr McFadden said to Selina. 'Yer Pa and Doctor Dinwiddie. I've been thinking . . .'

'Of having a telephone?'

'Wouldnae ken how to use the danged thing. No, when ye go hame tonight, will ye tak Lady?'

'Would she come?'

'She will if I tell her but mebbe, first time, ye'd better put her on a string.' Lady did not have a lead. 'Let her follow Haggis,' said Mr McFadden. 'Tak her to yer hoose. Show her. Tell her where she is. Maybe yer mither will let ye give her a piece – a bit of meat, oatcake or the like. I doot if Lady will eat it but it would show her she was with friends. Then let her off the string and tell her "Hame".'

'I'll take her over the road.'

'She'll tak hersel' ower the road – she kens. If we dae this yince or twice,' said Mr McFadden, 'then . . .'

63

'Lady will be the telephone.' Selina was delighted. 'And if anything happened . . .'

'I could send her with a note.'

'She wouldn't need a note,' said Selina. 'We should understand.'

Haggis still bustled up the lane but, going home at dark, Mr McFadden let them go down through the turnip field to the fields below it, and Haggis stood while Selina opened and shut the gates. 'Because he knows they're Mr McFadden's,' she told Ma. That evening Selina was proud because Lady did not need a string but came, trotting beside Haggis, looking up into Selina's face every now and then. 'She's certainly a beautiful dog,' said Ma, and Muffet gave her a bit of her own shortbread. Then Selina took Lady to the gate, said 'Home' and watched until the collie became a black speck skirting the turnip field.

Before she had gone. Selina had fastened a note to her collar, 'To train her,' said Selina. The note said, *Good nite* – Selina could never spell. Below was a cross for a kiss. It was the first kiss Mr McFadden had had since he was a boy. 'Tish-Tosh!' said Mr McFadden, but he did not put the note in the fire: he put it in his pocket.

4

Coming out to feed Big Wullie, his wives and the ducks and hens and shut them up for the night, Selina paused in the farmyard one evening to look over the hills. It was so quiet she could catch the hum of the tractor where Pa drove it up the high field; from where Selina stood it looked like a toy, Pa a dark dot. Along the edge of the forest, on the rowan trees the berries were turning red, the heather on the hills was nearly over, bracken too beginning to dry. 'Summer is drawing oot,' said Mrs Bridie.

Well, it's the end of August, thought Selina and, standing there with the scoop in her hand, another thought came as a shock. 'Selina never knows anything until it's right on her,' as Muffet said. Tomorrow, or was it the day after, school would begin.

'It's time I learned to look after mysel',' said Mr M'Fadden when she told him, but his eyes looked more tortoise-like than ever as he blinked. 'Don't ye gan thinking I can't get on without ye,' he said.

'You can use your foot better now,' Selina agreed but somehow that had ceased to be the point. 'I can come up after school ... but there's Brownies and dancing,' she said slowly, 'and I have to look after Haggis, and soon it will be dark by teatime. Oh dear!' said Selina.

Tim was flatly rebellious. 'What's the use of my going to school? I can't read and I can't write. What can I do there?'

'Stop that nonsense.' Mr McFadden said it sharply. 'I was *kept* from school to help on the farm.'

'Ah!' said Tim longingly.

'I minded. Do you want to grow up an ignorant like me?'

'Yes,' said Tim. 'Why can't we stay here, just us?'

'Us?' said Mr McFadden.

'Yes, you and me and Selina – and Lady and Big Wullie. Us.'

'Us,' repeated Mr McFadden. Selina saw his tortoise eyes blink and, 'We'll come up after school, Tim,' she said briskly, then faltered, 'Could we sometimes have our tea with you, Mr McFadden?'

'If ye must,' said Mr McFadden.

'We'll have tattie scones and bacon, just like now,' said Selina, cheering up. 'I know Ma will let me come at weekends. Autumn's the best time, Tim,' she tried to cheer him too. 'At the end there's Christmas. November fifth perhaps there'll be a bonfire. Pa says Scots people are beginning to keep Guy Fawkes Day and before that there's Hallowe'en.'

> Listen, listen, listen, listen
> Glisten, glisten, glisten, glisten.

The first morning that Muffet and Selina got their school bags ready, summer still lingered, but soon there were autumn colours; the leaves had already turned but now they began to fall, fluttering from the trees. The days were shortening, house lights shone early and, in the mornings, those unexplained cobwebs appeared on lawns and bushes and, once again, Selina asked, 'Where are the spiders?' There were mists and haziness; it was nearly witching time, but the spell of

66

autumn this year was broken in Menoock by troubles.

There was a meeting in the village, 'About our Park,' said Muffet. It seemed it was not to be 'our Park'. 'The man won't move,' Pa came home and told Ma. 'He *will not move*.' Even Selina, who seldom took much notice of outside affairs, could see the grown-ups were worried. 'Dang him,' said Mrs Bridie. 'I'd like to hang him.'

'Who?' asked Selina, but the talk went on over her head.

'It seems wrong,' said Ma, 'that one man should go against the good of the whole village.'

'That's the way it is,' Mrs Bridie said in wrath.

'It's his land.' Pa was trying to be fair, but he walked up and down the sitting room in his distress. 'It's his land.'

'But he has no use for it.'

'No farmer likes to part with his land.'

'It seems,' said Mr Doherty to the school, 'that the idea of the Park will have to be put aside for the now.'

'Why?' There was a chorus of 'why's', spoken and unspoken through the whole school.

'It's not an affair for bairns.'

'But it is. We were going to have the playground and the swimming pool.'

'Just because,' said Elspeth vindictively, 'that old beast won't sell the field.'

'What old beast? Who? Who?'

'Selina, you never know anything.'

'But who?'

'Mr McFadden.'

'Mr McFadden?' Selina was dazed.

'Yes. Your Mr McFadden, if you want him.'

'I don't believe it,' said Selina.

'If you don't, go and ask him, since you know him so well.' Though it was only afternoon break, Selina went.

'You're not *that* Mr McFadden?'

Selina had found him hobbling across the turnip field to look at the calves. She put herself between him and the gate. 'That Mr McFadden?'

'It's what they say.' Mr McFadden seemed unperturbed but Lady's tail sank down at the rasp in his voice.

'Who won't sell us our field?' Selina's blue eyes blazed like an angry kitten's.

'*Mae* field,' said Mr McFadden.

'When everybody wants it, everybody needs it, you won't let them have it?'

'Whae is this everybody?'

'People,' said Selina. Now tears were beginning to come. 'Don't you understand?' she blazed, in spite of the tears. 'You have Drumlarach, these hills and fields and forests. Old Mrs Muir, in the village, she hasn't a strip of garden. She can't walk to the fields, or the river or up the glen. There's nowhere she can go out. How would you like that?' asked Selina. 'You wouldn't keep Lady tied up in a kennel.'

'That's enough,' said Mr McFadden, and he blazed in his turn. 'Get oot of m' sicht.'

'I'm getting,' said Selina, 'and I'm never coming back. Never, never, never.'

It was Pa who found Selina in the shed with Haggis; her face and eyes were so swollen with tears that she could not come out. 'Why do I like all the wrong people?' wept Selina.

'Who is wrong?' asked Pa. He sat down on the bales of hay and drew Selina towards him. 'Let's think,' said Pa. 'If we were Mr McFadden – he has lived for his land, lived on it, worked for it, given up for it.'

'Not that bit,' said Selina.

'That bit too. There was a time when the McFaddens had no land, when they were just crofters and, after all, Menoock has existed for hundreds of years without a Park.'

'There were no cars then,' said Selina. 'Mrs Bridie says she can remember when, on summer evenings, people sat outside in the village street. Now they would be run over. How can they do that now?'

'They can't,' Pa agreed, 'but Mr McFadden doesn't understand that. After all, he hardly goes into the village, and is there a house where he has ever been invited in?'

'That's his fault.'

'Maybe, but if he's a crabby old cuss, he is. Come,' said Pa, getting up.

'Come where?' sniffed Selina.

'I'm going up to Drumlarach to give an eye to those calves. You had better come too.'

'I told him I was never coming back.'

'All the same, I think I should come if I were you,' said Pa.

'Changed yer mind?' asked Mr McFadden.

'There's Big Wullie and the hens to see to – and you haven't fed Lady.'

Mr McFadden did not say he did not feel like eating but the tin of corned beef was unopened. 'There's not only you at Drumlarach,' said Selina severely, handing him the tin opener while Lady wagged her tail so fast it seemed it might come off; and, that evening, something happened that Selina had not imagined could happen at Drumlarach: when it was time for her to go and Lady, as usual, came with her, suddenly Big Wullie opened his wings, squalled at his wives as if to tell them to stay where they were, stretched his big white neck and hurried after Selina, 'as if he wanted to show me he was glad I came back,' she told Pa, and soon he was strutting proudly beside her and Lady – 'seeing me home!' said Selina. Though he would not come over the road, he waited for Lady and, watching the two of them, black and white, making their way up through the fields, Lady with the customary good night note under her collar, Selina was glad she had taken Pa's advice.

Selina loves Mr McFadden. It was chalked in big letters on the playground wall. At morning break everybody shunned her; Selina spent the time playing ball with Tim but that afternoon, in the playground, they surrounded her.

'Who goes to see Mr McFadden?'

'Who goes up to Drumlarach?'

'Who rides her pony up there and pretends it goes by itself?'

'Pony! It's a miserable cuddie,' and, 'Selina Russell's Mr McFadden's pet,' they chanted. 'Mr McFadden's pet,' and they began to close in.

To begin with they only twitched Selina's coat and pulled her hair; then they began to punch and the hair tugs grew fiercer. Selina tried to stand still but they jostled and pushed her. Then some began to throw sand from the playground sand-pit. Selina had not known sand could hurt; it went into her eyes and stung them and down her mouth so that she choked; it was down her coat collar and in her hair. Tim's class must have come out because she was aware of him standing behind her; though his own hair came in for some fierce pulling and sand was thrown at him too, he still stood until they took him and tied him upside down by his braces to the school railings. 'That for your old McFadden,' they called.

Muffet saw them from the classroom window – the older boys and girls had different times for breaks and her seat was by the window; Muffet did not wait a moment. 'Excuse me, I have to go,' she said to the astounded Mr Doherty and, next moment, she was in the playground, scattering Selina's class and the others watching. Mr Doherty did not interfere.

'You scum. You little devils,' scolded Muffet, dealing hard slaps and cleaning Selina down, holding a hand-kerchief to her eyes. 'You, Rob, and you, Kirsty, untie Tim Scobie *at once*. His head will burst and you'll be sent to *prison*,' threatened Muffet. 'Selina's my sister and if you touch her, or him, again I'll call the big ones out; *then* you'll see,' said Muffet. 'We'll tie you up on the seesaw and bump you up and down. We'll put you head first into the sand-pit and see how *you* like the sand!'

They shrank away and Muffet took Selina and Tim into the cloakroom and tried to wash their eyes. There she was not sympathetic. 'See what you get us into with your Mr McFadden.'

'What's happened to yer faces?' Mr McFadden asked Selina and Tim that evening.

'We had . . . a sort of tumble,' said Selina. Well, Ma called fights 'rough and tumble'. 'A tumble in the playground.'

'What? The baith of ye?'

'I didn't tumble. I stood.' Tim said it proudly. Mr McFadden darted a suspicious look at them from his tortoise eyes.

'The others didnae get at ye?'

'They did.' Tim said it before Selina could stop him.

'Why?' Mr McFadden's face had its most forbidding expression; Selina could see he was getting angry and hastily she used Ma's phrase. 'We're not popular, Tim and I,' and, to reassure Mr McFadden, she said, 'We never have been.'

Drumlarach these days was extraordinarily quiet; Lady and Big Wullie kept lifting their heads as if listening for voices.

'Fool-bodies,' scolded Mr McFadden. 'It was a whaup,' but he found himself listening too. 'I keep thinking I hear voices,' he told Selina. 'Must be going daft.'

Selina did not think it at all queer. 'It's almost October – spunkie time,' she said.

'Ye young know-alls, nowadays, don't believe in spunkies.'

'I do,' said Selina.

'But what are they?' asked Tim.

'A kind of fairy; in England they call them will-o-the-wisps. You see a light, it moves and you can never catch it but you have to follow it because it's a spell. You hear a voice and you think it's an echo . . .'

'Or a whaup,' said Mr McFadden.

'But I think it's a spunkie. They come out at Hallowe'en.'

'Cross your heart?' asked Tim.

'I think they do.'

'Are they good or bad ones?'

'Both,' said Selina.

It was certainly a spunkie-haunted time for Mr McᶜFadden, and they were bad. 'Wicked,' said Mr McᶜFadden and set his lips. Doctor Dinwiddie, oddly silent with Mr McᶜFadden, had taken the foot out of plaster. 'I can drive the tractor now. See to things mysel'.'

'I don't think you will,' said Doctor Dinwiddie. 'You'll even want that plaster back.'

'How on airth?'

'Because now the real pain begins. The muscles have to lose their stiffness and they are inflamed and tender. You have to use them, work them, but it will hurt, every time you walk or move.' It did hurt; every step was torture. 'Lord! it's like walking on knives,' Mr McᶜFadden was betrayed once into saying as sweat broke out on his forehead and neck.

'You must go to the hospital every day for therapy,' the doctor told him.

'I'm not gan back.'

'Don't be silly, man. You will be lame for life.'

'Mebbe.'

'I'll have you taken and fetched.'

'I'm not gan back.'

Doctor Dinwiddie lost patience. 'Then you'll have to fight it out alone.'

'Aye.' Mr McᶜFadden was grim. It was a fight; his days were long, filled with pain – and lonely.

'Ma says now it's dark I mustn't come up after school,' Selina lamented.

'Yer mither's right.'

'She isn't.' Selina was rebellious. 'Look, I should be perfectly safe with the animals. Haggis and Lady and Big Wullie.'

'A spunkie might get ye.'

Selina shook her head. 'I know a charm,' and she recited:

> 'From elves, hobs, and fairies,
> That trouble our dairies,
> From fire drakes and fiends,
> And such as the devil sends,
> Defend us, good Heaven!'

'Wish I kent a charm,' said Mr McFadden. It was not only the foot and the pain – it was Menoock; the grocer mysteriously ran out of tins of stewed steak and corned beef. 'We're not stocking Sobranie tobacco any more,' they told Selina at the Post Office and her, 'Where'll I get it then?' only met with a shrug, and in the bakery, 'Mrs Allen can only spare one loaf,' reported Selina.

'Yin loaf for a *week*?'

'Aye.'

'What's the maiter wi' them?' asked Mr McFadden and Selina, embarrassed, looked at the ground. She knew but was not going to tell.

There was no diesel for Mr McFadden's tractor and his cattle cake was not delivered – Pa had to fetch it. Pa himself was put off the Committee for the Park. 'Just because I gave him a hand with his beasts. I'm a near neighbour,' and Pa exploded to Ma, 'Do they think I'm made of stone?'

'No, but they think Mr McFadden is.'

Ma had a note from him: *Madam. If you have occasion to go into town I shall be obliged if you would get a few things for me. I have decided not to shop in the village any more.*

Decided not to shop, and Ma said, 'Poor proud solitary old man.'

'Mr McFadden, would you give us each a turnip?'

'What on airth would ye be da'en wi' a neep?'

'I think you know,' said Selina. 'You know it's Hallowe'en.'

'Hallowe'en,' echoed Tim. His eyes were bright as he thought of it.

'Never heard of it,' said Mr McFadden.

'You have.' Selina was unperturbed. 'There's no one in Scotland who hasn't and you know what we do with the turnips.' Tim could not be expected to know – 'Because he hasn't been here,' said Selina. 'We hollow them out,' she told Tim. 'Hollow and scoop them out – that's hard work, then we cut holes for eyes and a mouth, little ones for nostrils if we can. Some people give them paper teeth and red rag tongue. On Hallowe'en night we put a lit candle in them or a nightlight, and carry them as a lantern or put them on gateposts. 'They look *horrible*,' said Selina with a shudder of pleasure, and she told Mr McFadden, 'I'm sure you did that when you were a boy.'

'Caertainly not. Neeps were for eating, not nonsense.'

'It isn't nonsense; they frighten witches and ghosts away.'

'And spunkies,' said Tim. 'Didn't you dress up like Selina says,' he asked Mr McFadden, 'dress as a witch or a ghost or a cat, something frightening? Selina says when it's dark we'll go round to people's homes and they have to let you in – even me,' said Tim. 'Then we sing a song or ask a riddle. Selina's going to teach me one and I'll get nuts and *tablet*,' Tim said that reverently.

'In m' day,' said Mr McFadden, 'bairns were not allowed to go round bothering folk and making a nuisance of themsel's.'

'Oh, they were,' said Selina. 'Mrs Bridie says when she was little all the children went. Now most of them stick at home watching television, but it's far more exciting out in the dark. The big boys and girls are always ghosts and they try and frighten you. It's gorgeous. Mrs Bridie always went. She's the same old as you,' said Selina. 'Why didn't you?'

'Because I wasnae let,' Mr McFadden said it curtly.

'Didn't you come back home and have champers?'

'I did not. What is champers?'

'Hallowe'en food. Potato and cheese all mashed together and put in the oven. Scrumptious! Didn't your mother make it for you?'

'Never kent mi mither.' Mr McFadden's tone was shorter still.

'But . . . didn't anyone ever give you even a toffee apple?'

'Never tasted yin.'

'I never tasted one either, but this year I'm going to,' said Tim. 'Champers as well. Selina says so.' He had absolute faith in Selina.

'Why shouldn't Mr McFadden?' Selina did not say that aloud but then and there she decided that Mr McFadden must share Hallowe'en – at long last, thought Selina. It only took another moment for her to

see that, to conjure up this, she must become a witch –
a good witch with a wand, thought Selina.

A good witch was needed in Menoock; the anger
against Mr McFadden was burning and soon it smoul-
dered too against the Russells. Mrs Bridie was loyal
but, 'I wish you had not taken up with him,' she told
Ma in sorrow. Muffet wished the same; after her threat
none of the children dared touch Selina or Tim in the
playground, 'But I doubt if the big boys and girls
would come out and help me now,' said Muffet. She
could defend Selina when Selina was at school but
now, in the lanes, stones were thrown at her and
Haggis. One cut Haggis on the leg, 'And Mr McFad-
den saw it – at once,' Selina told Ma.

'Dirty cowards!' exploded Mr McFadden and he told
Selina, 'Ye had better no bring Haggis up the lane.'

'I can't stop him.' Haggis, Selina knew, would come
no matter how many stones.

It was then that Mr McFadden tried to drive Selina
away from Drumlarach. 'Ye're no tae come here ony
mair,' he told her on Saturday. 'Ye and that pesty wee
boy. I've had enough of bairns and I dinnae need ye.'

'Do you not? You can't even walk as far as the barn!'
Selina's blue eyes saw straight through Mr McFadden
and she came next day.

'Are ye deef?' asked Mr McFadden.

'Yes,' said Selina.

Tim's aunt, Mrs Scobie, came to see Ma. 'Your little
girl's too rough, Mrs Russell. I can't get out of Tim
where she takes him but he comes back at all hours –
today with a cut on his cheek. That's too much.'

'I think it is,' said Ma.

'It isn't as if he were my own child, but he's my responsibility. I don't want to be unkind. I know I am particular.' Mrs Scobie smoothed her not over-clean skirt and tossed her head so that her earrings jangled, and Ma had a vision of Tim's outsize shirt, his stained old ragged trousers, the braces held together with string, his mud-caked broken boots but, 'I can't allow it,' said Mrs Scobie.

'Very well,' said Ma. 'I'll tell Selina. You tell Tim.'

There was a pause then, 'It would be better if you told him, Mrs Russell.'

Ma shook her head. 'I can't do that. Tim is always welcome here. Both Selina and he will be sad but, as you say, he's your responsibility. May I offer you some tea, Mrs Scobie?'

'Is that all you have to say?' Mrs Scobie asked indignantly.

'That is all,' said Ma.

Mr M‘Fadden sent a note to Ma. *Madam. Will you kindly stop your Selina coming here. I do not want her.*

'How can I?' Ma asked Pa. 'If I stopped Selina, she wouldn't forgive me – and I can't believe anyone in Menoock would hurt her.'

Pa was not so sure. Stones had been thrown into the farmyard, too. 'The cowards darenae come in because of Big Wullie,' Mr M‘Fadden exploded. 'I tell ye, if yin of m'birds or beasts are hurt, I shall call the police.'

'That wouldn't help,' said Pa. He had taken Mr M‘Fadden's tractor to the garage to get a gasket replaced and been refused. 'Take it to town,' said Mr Ross of the garage. 'Get that Sobranie tobacco in? It

doesn't pay us,' the postmistress said to Ma's face. Ma
did the shopping now and, 'I've no steak or corned beef
or milk for Drumlarach,' the grocer told her.

'They're trying to tire me oot,' said Mr McFadden.
'They'll no manage.'

5

It was told in the village afterwards that Menoock had never seen such an eerie night as that Hallowe'en. Mist came down early and so thick that, 'I dinnae ken if I should let you oot,' said Mrs Bridie. Mrs Bridie had kindly come to be in the house because Pa and Ma had gone to a meeting. 'A meeting on *Hallowe'en*!' Selina was astonished.

'Hallowe'en's not important to a grown-up,' Muffet told Selina.

'Then I'll never be a grown-up,' vowed Selina.

Mrs Bridie had promised to make champers – 'Make lots,' begged Selina – she would cook sausages too and make cocoa. 'What a mixture!' Pa had said but, 'Gorgeous!' said Selina.

Ma had left big bowls of nuts and apples, a plate of toffee apples – Muffet and Selina had spun them with toffee the night before and now they were crisp and hard. They were set ready in the hall and, 'If other children come to the house you will give them these, won't you?' Selina begged Mrs Bridie.

'Aye,' said Mrs Bridie. 'But I doot if many will be oot.' She peered through the window at the mist. 'It's gie coming up thick.'

'It makes it more mysterious,' said Selina and, indeed, as, one after the other, turnip lanterns were lit on gateposts and window-sills up and down the village, they looked splendidly grotesque. The wind in the trees sounded like witches keening and set the candles flickering so that the heads seemed alive.

Muffet's bat was frightening. Ma had made her wings from an old umbrella and when Muffet lifted her arms the wings opened, boned and pointed like a real bat's; her claws were yellow gloves but the rest of her was black and she had a black hood with a mask; her bat cry was so shrill Selina did not like to go near her.

For once, Selina was the pretty one. Mrs Bridie had brushed her hair to a sheen of gold; her pink dress and white apron were crisp and fresh; the red cloak matched her tights and shoes; she had a little pink mask but, best of all, was her hat, pointed and brimmed as witches' hats are, but rose-pink. Ma had stuck it with gold paper stars and there was a star on the end of her wand. 'My! You ought to bring us all luck with that,' said Mrs Bridie.

They were ready to go when Muffet pounced. 'You don't take a basket *full* for Hallowe'en.'

'Mind your own business,' said Selina gruffly.

'You little silly! You don't take people things; they give them to *you*. You need an *empty* basket.'

'This is a different basket.'

It was becoming a tug of war with Muffet and Selina both holding the basket. 'Let's see what you have there,' Mrs Bridie intervened. 'For the peace sake,' she would have said. 'Tablet,' said Mrs Bridie. 'Two toffee-apples, nuts . . .'

'Trust Selina,' said Muffet, 'to get things the wrong way round.'

'I haven't,' protested Selina. 'Look, I have an empty basket as well.'

'Are you sure you have it richt, Selina?' Mrs Bridie was anxious to be fair. Selina could only nod.

'She's going to take them to her precious Haggis or some nonsense like that,' but there was Elspeth – or

Eleanora – as a black, black witch come to distract Muffet's – or Marguerite's – attention and, with her, a bevy of other girls as goblins, ghosts, a cat, even a rowan fairy and, 'I told you they would be out,' Muffet told Mrs Bridie.

I wonder what Tim is doing? thought Selina. She ached when she thought about Tim; it seemed a long long time since she had seen him. Perhaps he had managed to keep enough pennies to buy one of the village shop masks. Ma said they were ugly but what else could Tim do? His aunt would never bother to dress him up and, since she had come to see Ma, Selina was not allowed near Tim; even in school they were in different classes.

'Dinnae bide oot ower lang now and mind, go only in the village.' Selina shut her ears to Mrs Bridie's parting commands. 'I'm away to the kitchen now to make your champers,' she shouted from the front door. 'Come back while it's guid and hot.'

If the mists were thick in the village, they were thicker at Drumlarach. Owls were hooting in the lane at three o'clock that afternoon; the farm seemed eerie – and uneasy. Lady was restless and Big Wullie cackled and pecked his wives unmercifully. When Mr McFadden had finished his early supper, and Lady hers, and he had made up the fire, meaning to sit comfortably and smoke his pipe, he could not do it; he felt too lonely. It was a new feeling for Mr McFadden, 'But it had been coming on for some time,' he told Ma afterwards. Strange! he had always taken it for granted he should be alone. Now he kept going to the front door.

'I shan't be coming to see you this week,' Selina had told him. 'I shall be too busy.' She had not meant to be unkind. It will be all the more surprise for him, she had thought, but now Big Wullie and the geese and the fowls were shut in their pens and the yard was silent. Down below in the village there would be stifled shrieks of laughter, pretended screams, light from the turnip lanterns. For a moment Mr McFadden had a mind to go and cut two turnips, hollow them and carve them and set them at Drumlarach gate. 'But naebody will come up here,' he told himself. He could hear Selina telling Tim, 'We go into people's houses – they have to let us – and sing or ask them riddles. They guess who we are and give us goodies.' Mr McFadden had no goodies to give; he had not even heard the word for a long long time.

He shut his door and went back to his chair and he did not light his pipe and, if a tough old farmer can have the same feeling as a young girl, Mr McFadden felt like Cinderella when she could not go to the ball; but he was tired. 'Walkin' a' day on that foot tires me oot,' he told Lady and presently Mr McFadden was fast asleep.

Big Wullie set up a cackling in his pen. Lady raised her head, listened and ran to the door. 'Quiet,' said Mr McFadden. He said it in his sleep. Lady ran to him, back to the door and whined for permission to bark. He did not hear her.

Figures in white robes had crept up on Drumlarach; silently, except for smothered laughter, they fetched Mr McFadden's ladder and stealthily placed it against the house. Two shrouded figures went up it and one, agile and quiet, crept, without shoes, over the slates while the second hauled and passed up something heavy, dark and damp. Next moment, 'God Almighty! Lord! Help me. Lord!' shouted Mr McFadden.

The fire seemed to have blown out into the room; smoke was billowing down the chimney, smarting Mr McFadden's eyes, choking his mouth and nose. He struggled to the door where Lady stood barking; out in the air he staggered and stood, holding to the wall, choking and spluttering. 'Is the danged chimney on fire?' Yet, though smoke was rolling through the door, Mr McFadden could see no flames and Lady had rushed round the side of the house in a fury of barking; but when Mr McFadden came round there was no sign of anyone, only the ladder standing against the house wall and, from the lane, that smothered laughing.

Mr McFadden hobbled back to the yard and let out Big Wullie; the great gander ran hissing to the gate but there was no one there either. The whole farmhouse was filling with smoke. 'What am I to do?' cried Mr McFadden.

An answer came hurtling in from the lane; another figure, but so small it did not reach the gateposts, had arrived; it wore a flapping nightdress, once white, now wet and dirty, and its face was hidden by one of the village masks so lurid and hideous that, for once in his life, Big Wullie ran away. The figure flung itself on Mr McFadden. 'It's Tim, Sir. Tim. Och! I thought I could be in time.'

Tim was gasping and sobbing as he tore off his mask. 'I had to wear this so they wouldn't know who I was. I tried to get here first.'

Mr McFadden held him while he sobbed. 'Whae are "they", Tim? Whae?'

'The big boys,' Tim gasped. 'Och! Mr McFadden. They've put a turf on your chimney.'

'So that's what 't'is. I thought the hoose was on fire.' Mr McFadden did not swear; he let Tim go and, for a moment, it seemed he would sink into the ground. Then he straightened up. 'Timothy.'

'Sir.'

'Take this claes-prop.' He picked up a tall pole from the yard. 'Come wi' me,' and he took Tim through the smoke to the ladder. 'Do ye think, Tim, ye could get up there?'

'It's mortal high,' said Tim.

'This cursed foot!' groaned Mr McFadden. 'Come, Tim. I'll hud the ladder and hand ye up the pole. Then ye only have to get to the stack and see can ye no push the turf off. Will ye try?'

'I will that,' said Tim.

'Dinnae look down.' Mr McFadden was anxious. Tim was up the ladder, that was not difficult but, in climbing over the slates, he had to carry the pole, and Mr McFadden had to watch the small figure slithering and falling and cursed his own helplessness again. Then, 'I'm by the stack,' piped Tim.

'Guid lad.'

'It's awful dark.'

'Aye, but can ye see the turf?'

'Yes. What'll I do now?'

'Can ye stand up?'

Silence. Mr McFadden could just see the small white figure standing precariously up.

'I'm up. What'll I do now?'

'Can the pole reach?'

Another silence. Then, 'Just.'

'See can ye no push the thing off.' Mr McFadden could hear the pole scraping and pushing.

'It's too . . . heavy,' panted Tim.

'God Almighty. Tim, ye had better come down.'

'Down. I'm going up.'

'Not on yer life,' thundered Mr McFadden. 'Timothy, I forbid ye. Ye are not to climb the stack,' but the pole came rattling over the slates and rolled down on the ground by Mr McFadden. 'Tim, never mind the smoke. Come you doon. *Tim!*' but, through the mist and smoke seeping from under the turf, he could see the little white shape climbing up the stack; he could hear Tim breathing. 'Them big boys did it,' called Tim. 'So can I!'

'Their arms are longer and their legs. Ye're too wee,' but, 'Hoots!' called Tim, 'there's a rail,' and soon he had climbed the stack. 'There's a terrible smell of smoke. I'm choked,' he shrieked, then did almost choke and knew it was wise not to open his mouth. His eyes were streaming but, standing with his feet apart on two infinitesimal ledges of granite, holding to the rail with one hand, with the other he pushed with all his might. For a moment he thought it was true, he was too small, but slowly the big turf moved, crumbling at the edges. Tim steadily pushed though sweat started out on his forehead and neck, and his eyes, mouth and nose were full of smoke; his fingers holding to the rail felt as if they were being torn off, his feet were slipping, but he pushed until suddenly, and so unexpectedly that it put Tim off balance, the turf slid off the chimney pot and fell with a thud on to the roof slates below; the prisoned smoke billowed out and Tim came over backwards, fell on the slates, bounced and rolled over and over down the roof, bounced again off the gutter and was caught in Mr McFadden's arms below. The pain that gave Mr McFadden's foot made him cry out but he held Tim safely.

'Son, are ye hurt?' Mr McFadden set him down still holding him. Tim was winded and it was a few moments before he could speak. Then, 'I . . . don't . . . think . . . I . . . am.' Tim was feeling himself all over and said in wonder, 'I'm still together.'

'Ye must be made of inja rubber,' but Mr McFadden's voice dwindled. 'Tim, I'm feart I micht faint.'

'You can't faint here,' said Tim firmly. 'There's nothing to faint on,' which sensible remark brought Mr McFadden round.

'Ye're right,' said Mr McFadden.

When at last the smoke had cleared and they could get into the house and Mr McFadden had made up the fire, he saw that Tim was shivering. 'Get oot of they claes. I have a jersey and socks ye can put on while I dry these.' Tim was as shy and independent as Mr McFadden himself. 'Turn your back,' he said sternly and Mr McFadden obeyed.

The jersey almost swallowed Tim, 'But it's beautiful warm,' he said; the socks stretched up his thighs, and inches in front of his feet. Never seen a boy so thin and white, thought Mr McFadden. Legs like pea-sticks, and, 'Are ye hungry?' he asked.

'Och! I am.'

'I thought they stuffed ye with sweet stuff and nuts on Hallowe'en.'

'I did have a bagful, but . . .'

88

'But?'

'I dropped them. It was the hurry, you see.'

'Ae see,' said Mr M⁽ᶜ⁾Fadden. 'Coming up to warn me. Humph! I must try and make it up to ye.' He had not much to make it up with but he opened a tin of steak. The smell as he warmed it made Tim's nostrils twitch and he ate a whole plateful, scouring it round with a piece of bread until Mr M⁽ᶜ⁾Fadden thought the enamel would come off. 'Seems you hadnae much inside ye,' he said. 'Did that aunt of yours no give ye ony tea?'

'Not today,' said Tim.

'That's iniquitous.'

'Some days she does.' Tim said it hastily. 'Some – well, she forgets.'

'Too bad,' said Mr M⁽ᶜ⁾Fadden and he meant '*too bad!*'

'Yer claes are dry now,' he said when Tim had licked the last crumb of bread. 'If ye can ca' them claes.'

'It's my auntie's nightgown. She doesn't know I took it. I'll get lammed,' said Tim.

'Ye'd better away hame,' but Tim was swaying on his feet. 'Come away, son.'

'I don't think I can,' said Tim.

'But yer aunt . . .'

'She's at t'pub and so is uncle. They'll not miss me till the morning; even then, most days I'm away to school before they've woken up.'

'Without any breakfast.' Mr M⁽ᶜ⁾Fadden was grim.

'Aye,' but Tim could not talk about that now; he gave a great yawn. 'Mr M⁽ᶜ⁾Fadden, Sir – I think – I must go to sleep . . .' and he dropped down and curled himself on the sheepskin rug.

'Not on t'floor in all them draughts.'

'I always sleep on the floor.' Tim gave another huge yawn. 'Always sleep on the floor.'

'Not here you don't. Get up on the sofy.'

'*Me!* On your sofy!' For a moment Tim's eyes opened wide but before Mr McFadden could put him there, Tim was fast asleep.

Mr McFadden, sitting in his armchair, deep in thought, was roused by the sound of a car, by Big Wullie cackling and Lady's bark. He went to the door as two policemen strode into the yard. So Tim's aunt and her man have missed him, thought Mr McFadden.

'Sorry to disturb you, Mr McFadden,' the older policeman said stiffly, 'but have any Hallowe'en children called on you?'

'Called on me!' Mr McFadden's wrath boiled over. 'If I could get m'hands on those young rascals . . .' The wrath mounted as he saw the younger policeman was laughing.

'Come, come, Mr McFadden, you must expect tricks on Hallowe'en.'

'Tricks! They almost set m'hoose on fire. Do you laugh at *that*?' and Mr McFadden spat on the ground by the policeman's feet.

'Easy, Bob,' said the older man to the young one and, to Mr McFadden, 'Hallowe'en is Hallowe'en, though this does seem to have gone beyond a joke, but it isn't children we're looking for, Mr McFadden, it's a child.'

'I have him here,' said Mr McFadden. 'He's asleep on m' sofy but ye had better tak him hame. Hame! What a word for it. I doot if ye'll find onybody there.

Ye can always dig them oot of the pub,' and he added, 'Maybe ye can manage nae tae wake him.'

'Him?' asked the policeman. 'A boy? But, Mr McFadden, the child we are looking for is a little girl.'

6

'Where's Selina?'

Muffet and her friends had come back, trooping into the kitchen, bringing the smell of mist and wet with them. Their faces were tingling with cold and excitement and each of them was carrying her 'loot', as Muffet called it, with her. 'What did you get?' 'What did they give you?' The questions rang as they took off hats and caps and discarded cloaks and sheets, broomsticks and masks, Muffet her umbrella wings. '*Look* at the tablet Sarah's got!' 'My toffee apples have stuck together.' 'I haven't any nuts,' wailed one. 'Hard cheese!' she was answered.

They crowded round the fire. 'Mrs Bridie, we're starving.' 'I didn't eat any tea on *purpose*.' 'I'm as thirsty as twenty ship-wrecked sailors, Mrs Bridie.'

'*Where's* Selina?'

For a moment there was a pause, a blank. Then, 'Isn't she here?' asked Muffet.

'She is not.'

'She must have gone upstairs.'

'She has not.'

The girls looked at one another, longing to get back to their chatter, above all have supper and, 'She hasn't come in yet, that's all,' said Muffet.

'You are supposed to keep an eye on your sister.'

'I was supposed to be having fun, not looking after Selina,' but, seeing Mrs Bridie's uncompromising face, Muffet added, 'You know what Selina is.'

'She's probably singing her head off in somebody's house,' said Elspeth.

'That's no like Selina.'

'She's forgotten the time,' which *was* like Selina but, 'Near eight o'clock,' said Mrs Bridie. 'All the bairns will have gone in by now.'

'She'll come,' said Muffet. 'Mrs Bridie, can't we have our champers?'

'You can bide.' Mrs Bridie was terse. 'I'm going up the village to ask at every hoose.'

'Wait,' said Muffet. 'I remember now. She had some fool idea of taking toffee apples to Haggis. You know how silly she is about him.'

'She wouldnae be this long. All the same, you gae doon tae the paddock and see, you and Elspeth.'

'*Now!* Oh, Mrs Bridie!'

'Do you no understand?' said Mrs Bridie. 'I'm responsible for you. Off with you now. Go and see.'

Selina was not in anyone's house and Haggis was not in the paddock.

'She couldn't have gone riding now in the dark,' said Muffet.

'She has. Her saddle's not there.' That was Elspeth.

'In this mist, she could be lost. Dear God!' said Mrs Bridie. Almost automatically, she was spooning out helpings of champers, pouring out cocoa. 'You might as well eat your suppers,' but somehow, to Muffet's surprise, she did not want any. 'You dinnae think,' Mrs Bridie paused, the jug in her hand, 'you dinnae think Selina could have gone up tae Mr M'Fadden?'

'He would have sent her back long ago. He always does, with Lady and Big Wullie.' In her worry, Muffet gave away what the Russells had kept secret. 'Besides,

Mr McFadden hates Hallowe'en. He told her it was a nonsense . . . but perhaps we should go and look,' said Muffet uncertainly.

'I'm not going up tae Drumlarach, not in this mist,' and Mrs Bridie said, 'I'm going tae tell the police.'

No one had noticed Selina go. At the last house but three she had slipped away and, in a few minutes, was in the shed with Haggis; she had taken the precaution of tying him up there. 'You have plenty of hay,' she had told him. She had taken his saddle and bridle down and her saddlebags. When Haggis was ready, she filled these from Mr McFadden's basket and led Haggis out of the shed, but now she came to it, Selina wavered; she was tired, cold and hungry; her excitement seemed to have waned.

The mist was thickening; behind it the hills were dark – the long lane would be eerie. Almost she went home, but she looked at her own basket; it was over-flowing with oranges, apples, sweets, nuts – though the village was so angry with the Russells, the women would not be unkind on Hallowe'en. She thought of the singing and laughter and guessing, and then of Mr McFadden, all alone and out of the fun at Drumlarach.

'He doesn't know what fun is,' she told Haggis. 'We'll ride up. I'll tap on the door with my wand and we'll ride straight in. Wait till you see his face when I show what we have for him,' and, 'We're going,' she told Haggis.

She had forgotten to bring a torch; 'Of course,' sighed Selina and, 'Can you see the way?' she whispered to Haggis, whispered because it was more than eerie in the lane, it was 'spookey', whispered Selina.

94

The very stones in the wall glimmered faintly when the mist parted – or glowered, thought Selina; they seemed to be closing in on her and Haggis as if they could crush us into the road, she thought. She had to ride under the thorn trees that overhung the lane with their bare knotted branches and she remembered how she had once thought that trees at night bent down and twisted their twigs in your hair to pull you up. 'But I have my witch's hat on,' she said to Haggis. 'They can't catch my hair.' That made her feel better but the next moment an owl's hoot close by made her start. It was so close it sounded like a human – or not a human, thought Selina. A cold shiver ran down her back and, 'I think we had better go back,' she said aloud, but Haggis was plodding on and she knew she could not stop him now.

It was then she saw lights – but there can't be lights in the lane. They were not car lights but little ones that danced and disappeared. Spunkies, thought Selina, and her skin seemed to creep at the back of her neck. Spunkies are not real but the lights were there, small sudden flashes that, yes, moved. Selina's heart seemed to be beating in her throat, her legs seemed frozen to Haggis's sides and her hands holding the reins were clammy.

> 'F-from fire-drakes and f-fiends,
> And such as the devil s-sends,
> Defend us . . .'

she quavered, but the charm did not seem to work. The lights were coming nearer.

Suddenly Haggis stopped, his ears pricked forward. He gave a whicker of alarm as over the wall, and

through a gap in its stones, came tumbling tall forms dressed in white robes and wearing masks. The masks were horrible, the forms made weird howls and hoots, shrieks and gabbling noises as they crowded round Selina and Haggis but, They're not spunkies. They're boys, thought Selina in relief.

The relief was short lived. 'And where do ye think ye're going, this time of the nicht?'

The boys were not bad, only 'drunk with mischief,' as Mrs Bridie was to say. After putting the turf on Mr McFadden's chimney, they had gone on far up the lane and how surprised was Major McBain to find, in the morning, a cow tied up in his hunter's stable, the hunter out in the field, 'Where he might have caught his death of chill,' said the Major in a fury. The farmer at Craigieburn found a litter of little pigs – 'We happed 'em in sacks so they didnae squeal,' said the boys – where his sow, due to farrow, had been penned; the sow herself was in the orchard spoiling the trees. Old Mrs Potterton had her front gate taken neatly off its hinges and laid across the front door, blocking it. The boys' blood was up and to meet the talked-about Selina Russell and her pony was an opportunity too good to miss.

'We ken where ye're off tae. Ye're going tae see old McFadden.' There were hoots of laughter. 'We've been to McFadden's.' That seemed to be a great joke though Selina could not see why. 'So why should ye be going?'

Selina was too bewildered to answer and one of them caught her arm and twisted it. 'Answer when ye're spoken to.'

'Ouch!' said Selina.

'Then answer.'

'I can't – when you're hurting me. Ouch!'

'Answer. Why are ye going?'

'For – Hallowe'en,' faltered Selina.

More guffaws. 'He's had his Hallowe'en.'

'He won't give ye onything,' they told her. 'Best go along hame, tiddler. Ye'll get naught oot of him.'

'I don't want to,' Selina said incautiously. 'I'm taking him Hallowe'en.'

'What are ye tak'n? Show.'

The boys were hungry and Selina knew if they set eyes on what was in her saddlebags there would be no toffee apples or nuts or tablet for Mr McFadden, and she set her heels so fiercely into Haggis's sides that he jumped; then, as if he understood, he started into a canter; at the same time Selina beat at the boys with her wand. One of them, Stuart Riddick, had taken off his mask and she caught him across the face. With a yell of anger he and the others chased her up the lane. But they can't catch us, thought Selina, and gave an owl hoot of defiance. They were surging nearer but she was at Drumlarach; she could see the house-lights across the farmyard and then she saw, too, that the gate was shut.

Haggis had to stop, his sides heaving, breath blowing heavily through his nostrils; he stood as Selina flung herself off his back. 'Quick! Quick!' she cried it aloud, but her hands were so cold that she fumbled at the chain and bolt. 'Quick!' but she was not quick enough. As the gate swung open, the boys were on her. Two of them gave Haggis such a belt that again he jumped and cantered off through the gate and into the farmyard, but Selina was borne backwards and dragged up the lane.

'Grease rat.'

'Not a grease rat.' Selina had to speak though she was so frightened now the words would not come properly. 'N-not a g-grease rat.'

'Y'are. All on ye. Yer Pa and Mither. Traitors,' and they all took up the cry. 'Traitors! Traitors!'

'We're not,' cried Selina. 'My Pa *wanted* the Park. He was on the Committee.'

'And was put off. Yer Mither makes cakes for yon old divil.'

'He's not a devil ... and my Pa ... my Ma ...' Selina tried to stop her sobs. 'You're ghastly mean boys.' The sobs grew louder.

'Ar, hold her whisht!' said a big boy, Ian Ross, and one of them clapped a hand over her mouth. It was the boy who had gone up the chimney and the hand smelled of soot. Selina choked and kicked and struggled. Then she bit the hand as hard as she could.

The boy yelled. 'Shush! Quiet!' the others hushed him.

'But she bit me. Little hell cat,' and he gave Selina a clout on the side of her head that knocked her sideways.

'Coo! She's drawn bluid.'

'I'm glad,' Selina managed to say. 'I'm glad.'

'Glad, are ye? We'll see,' and, 'Teach her a lesson,' they cried and, 'Let's tie her up,' said one.

'Yah. She bites like a dog. Treat her like a dog.'

'Tie her tae a tree.'

'With old Ma Potterton's clothes line.'

'I'll fetch it,' and next thing Selina knew she was bundled against a thorn tree and a rope was being wound round her. 'No! No!' shrieked Selina but the

rope was tight round her ankles, knees, waist and
shoulders, her arms tied down and,

> 'Pink hat! How's that?
> Pink hat! Hell cat!'

they chanted and cried, 'Noo go and see yer mouldy
Mr McFadden.'

Selina's despairing cries followed them down the
lane and then grew fainter. They meant to go back and
untie her but a fight broke out between Stuart and Ian
and they forgot the time.

When the two policeman had left Drumlarach, taking Tim with them – they had carried him wrapped in
the old red quilt, still sound asleep – Mr McFadden
was uneasy. Selina lost. 'Well, it's nothing tae dae wi'
me,' Mr McFadden told himself but, tell as he might, it
did not prevent him going to the door, opening it and
listening. Lady was strangely uneasy too, kept break-
ing into barking then whining. 'Quiet,' said Mr
McFadden. 'Hush noo. Quiet,' and quietened neither
of them while Big Wullie too, though shut now in his
pen, kept up an incessant noise. Each time Mr
McFadden opened the door the mist was thicker, but
broken by the wind into strange swirls and, in a gap
now and then, he could catch a glimpse of the fields
and hills, oddly star-lit. He could hear an owl's hoot. 'A
frightening nicht for a wee lassie to be oot,' he said to
Lady.

'But she can't be oot.' Coming back to the fire, he
worked himself up into anger. 'What are they thinking
of, her faither and mither? They are as bad as Tim's

aunt,' but he knew the Russells were not like that. 'It's this Hallowe'en,' muttered Mr McFadden. 'Letting bairns traike aboot in the dark. She'll be in by noo, surely.' He wished he could send Lady down with a note to ask but, 'It's nothing tae dae wi' me,' and, 'Why would she be here?' he asked indignantly. 'She's far too ta'en up wi' her Hallowe'en to think of Drumlarach. Not like wee Tim. Aye, I had best go tae bed,' and he hobbled to the door to bolt it for the night.

Once more he looked out and, as if at a signal, the mist parted and the stars shone over Drumlarach. Mr McFadden stood in the doorway, riveted; down in his turnip field was a small dark shape; it was Haggis and his saddle was empty.

It was only a dream, thought Selina, a bad dream. How could she, Selina, be trussed to a tree, foot to head, bound to this lonely thorn tree in the dark cold frightening night? It can't be true, thought Selina, but it was. As the cold woke her senses, the pain from the blow on her head throbbed and the rope was too tight round her ankles and knees and cut into her chest. If only someone would come. Pa and Ma would surely miss her; then Selina remembered Pa and Ma were out. Muffet and Mrs Bridie would have missed her; Selina knew they would go to look for her but how would they know where to look? Selina herself did not know where she was except that it was somewhere above Drumlarach. She tried to call; she called and called until her throat was hoarse and her own voice choked her. She had not known how uncomfortable it is to cry when your hands are not free to wipe your eyes and nose.

It must be the middle of the night, thought Selina. Then she heard the Menoock church clock strike nine o'clock. She grew colder and colder; the mist had seeped into her clothes and the rope was searing her legs and chest as she leant against it. She could no longer stand up by herself. 'Ma,' whispered Selina. 'Ma,' and, 'Please. Please. Please.'

Presently the pink hat drooped down over the ropes.

*

'Lady. Find Selina. Selina.'

At the sight of Haggis, Mr McFadden had stood, 'as if turned to stane,' he said afterwards. Now he knew why Big Wullie had kept cackling, why Lady barked and whined; it was only he who had not sensed. 'Dunderclunk that I am,' said Mr McFadden.

He called 'Se-lina. Sel-ina. Selina!' through cupped hands; the sound went so far into the night that it seemed to echo from the hills as if it were mocking him, 'Se-lina. Sel-ina.' Big Wullie hushed and lifted his head; Lady had hers on one side, her ears cocked listening; there was no answer but Haggis lifted his head too and came trotting up through the turnips to Mr McFadden. The little pony was wet, shivering like Tim, and lathered. 'Ye have had a fricht,' said Mr McFadden. Soothing and patting, he led him into the old stable, unbridled him and filled the manger with hay. He lifted off the saddle to rub Haggis down and, surprised to find it so heavy, opened the saddle-bags. 'Now what would she be doing bringing her goodies up here? Why was she riding at a'? Och, if only you could *speak*.' Haggis could not, but looked up at Mr McFadden with grateful eyes – what could be seen of them through forelocks – as he munched the hay. Again Mr McFadden called into the night but the only sound was Haggis's contented munching and, again, the hoot of an owl. Big Wullie and Lady seemed to be waiting, expectant, and 'I mun git a licht,' said Mr McFadden.

He hobbled back into the house and saw on the window-sill a grubby handkerchief that Selina had dropped, 'as usual,' Muffet would have said. It had lain there for a week but, 'Och!' said Mr McFadden again and gave it to Lady to sniff. 'Selina,' said Mr

McFadden and gave the shepherd whistle that meant 'Gae and find a lost sheep'. Lady darted out into the dark.

Mr McFadden would not use a torch. 'A lantern needs none of yer batteries and nonsense and gies a better licht,' but it took time to light it and now he grudged that time. When he came out Lady was gone. He whistled and she came back to him, urgently whining. Mr McFadden hobbled as fast as he could, Big Wullie behind him. Then Lady stopped; he held the lantern high and its light caught the glint of a gold paper star and – thought Mr McFadden, peering – could it be a hat? A hat, bent over from something small and wilting from a thorn tree. 'Selina,' he whispered. 'Selina.'

There was no answer, but Lady ran to her, whining.

'Hold me tight. Tight,' begged Selina.

She had opened her eyes to find herself lying where Tim had gone to sleep on the horsehair sofa – 'How Mr McFadden carried that lump of a child all that way with his foot so painful, I don't know,' said Ma afterwards – the good witch's finery lay in a small soaked heap on the sheepskin rug. Mr McFadden was rubbing Selina with a towel; Lady was anxiously licking her feet and Big Wullie, who had slipped inside, was craning his neck to see from the door – he knew better than to come further in. Selina was with her friends and she let the tears flow; Mr McFadden had never seen such tears.

'Noo, noo,' he said as he rubbed her until she tingled. Then he wrapped her in his blanket – Tim already had his quilt. Between sobs Mr McFadden fed

Selina spoon by spoon with milk; it was out of a tin –
all he had – but nothing could have been better than its
hot sweetness. It did not stop the tears though and, as
Mr McFadden bent anxiously over her, Selina's arms
went round his neck and she clung to him; he picked
her up, took her to the fire and sat down with her in the
armchair. 'There, there. Noo, noo.'

'But what I cannae understand,' he said when she
had quietened, and he had put her back on the sofa,
warm under the blanket, 'what I cannae understand is
what ye were doing up here when ye had had yer
goodies. Yer saddlebags were full of them.'

'They're not my goodies. They're yours.'

'Mine?'

'Yes. You have never . . .' *sniff, sob*, went Selina, 'had
any Hallowe'en . . .' *sniff* . . . 'Nor anything nice; no
wonder you're so nasty.' Selina was too far gone to spare
Mr McFadden's feelings. 'Oh! I wanted to surprise
you,' and the tears began again as she thought how
it had all been spoiled. Mr McFadden could just make
out the words 'toffee-apples' and 't-t-tablet'. 'I made
them for you . . . and that wasn't all. I was a good
witch on purpose even though they laughed.'

'Why should they laugh?'

'They always do, at me, but Mrs Bridie said,' *sob,
sniff*, 'on Hallowe'en night a witch can t-turn quite
good people into t-toads and so I thought . . .'

'Ye thocht?'

'Perhaps a good witch could make a nice p-person
from a g-gurney-faced old scunner.'

'So I'm a gurney-faced old scunner.'

'Of course.' Selina sat up, her blue eyes wide with
astonishment. 'Didn't you know?'

'I hae heard tell,' said Mr McFadden.

'But they threw my wand away. They beat Haggis and he had done nothing, nothing at all,' and Selina wailed, 'Where *is* Haggis?'

'Noo, noo.' Mr McFadden caught her as she was throwing off the blanket to go and look. 'Haggis is snug in the stable. Bide still,' and that was how Pa and Ma found her when they came.

'Selina's lost and it's all my fault. I should have kept my eye on her!' Muffet had flung herself on Ma almost before she and Pa were out of the car.

'Selina *lost*? She can't be.'

'She is.'

'Not in Menoock!'

'She is. She is.' Behind Muffet was Mrs Bridie, her face red and swollen with crying and, with her, Elspeth and a crowd of other girls. 'Och! I knew this would happen, letting them gae traiking oot in the dark . . .'

'They always go out for Hallowe'en, perfectly safely.'

'Safely, is it? The police dinnae think so.'

'The police!' Ma and Pa were pale now but Ma was still calm. 'Tell me exactly what happened.' At once there was a babel of voices, everyone talking together and at the top of their voices until, 'Quiet!' shouted Pa. 'All come into the house. Everybody. Now shut the door. Now, Muffet, tell us exactly what happened. *Only Muffet*,' but all Muffet could do was to sob, 'She's been gone hours and hours.'

'Not hours and hours,' said Ma. 'You didn't go out till after six and it's now – a quarter to ten. She can't have gone far. Mrs Bridie, please . . .'

'I cannae speak for trembling,' said Mrs Bridie and a

torrent of words came out, ending, 'Mrs Russell, I could kill mysel' thinking of that poor mite oot in the dark alone.'

'We don't know if she is in the dark, or that she's alone.'

'Please God, she is. We dinnae ken who has got hold of her.'

'Mrs Bridie!'

'The horrible stories yin hears.'

'*Mrs Bridie!*'

'I think she has been kidnapped,' began Elspeth when, 'Hush,' said Muffet suddenly. 'Listen.' They listened. It was a whining and a scratching at the back door. 'Lady!' Muffet was out of the room and down the passage in a flash. 'It *is* Lady,' she cried from the back door.

'There you see,' said Mrs Bridie in triumph. 'Dinnae I say the whole time that Selina was safe at Drumlarach?'

It was the first of November, the day after Hallowe'en and a misty morning, and Selina, none the worse, except for sore wrists and ankles, walked up to Drumlarach to fetch Haggis. 'Yer mither let ye come?' Mr McFadden said it in surprise when he saw her.

'Why not? They were only boys.' Selina was quoting Pa; in daylight she was brave but, for the rest of her life, she would remember the chase up the lane and the hours under the thorn tree. 'Not hours – perhaps an hour,' Ma corrected. 'It felt like hours,' said Selina. 'They were only boys,' she told Mr McFadden, 'and this morning Stuart and Ian came to *apologize*,' but Mr McFadden was brooding over what he had said to Ma

Mr McFadden's
Halloween

P 7

P 94

P

P

P

P

P

P

P

last night: 'They can throw stanes, at me, aye, and put turfs on m' chimney, but when it comes tae the bairns . . .' and he shuddered as he saw again Selina, unconscious and trussed to the thorn tree, Tim, braving the gang of big boys and struggling up the hill to warn him and, 'I dinnae ken what tae dae,' said Mr McFadden now. Then he burst out, 'Hoo can I sell that bluidy field withoot losing face?'

'The field for the Park?' asked Selina. 'But you won't sell it. You said so.'

'Aye, I swore it.' Mr McFadden ground the stone flags with his stick. 'Now look what ye and Timothy have done to me!'

'Us?' Selina stared at him with a puzzled face. 'We've done nothing.'

'Ye hae been done tae.' Mr McFadden would not explain more than that but burst out again. 'I dinnae want their auld money.'

'If you don't want it, don't take it.' Selina was beginning to understand. 'You said you wouldn't sell them the field.'

'Aye. Ower and ower again.'

'Then don't sell it.'

'Don't?'

'No. Give it,' said Selina.

'Gie it?' Mr McFadden seemed not to have heard that word before. 'Gie them mae field?'

'Aye. Then you won't have to take their auld money because you won't sell them the field – you'll give it. You won't lose your face,' and Selina said what Muffet would have called vulgar but exactly fitted the occasion, 'That will make them talk on the other side of theirs.'

7

'Good morning, Mr McFadden.'

'How are you, Mr McFadden?'

'I have your Sobranie tobacco in for you, Mr McFadden.'

'Would Lady welcome a bone?' Even, 'Well, Angus, how's things?'

'Aye. They're michty polite noo they hae what they wanted,' said Mr McFadden.

'It's not that. They like you because of what you have done.' Selina believed that but Mr McFadden put on his most tortoise-like look.

'This'll no make a hae'penny of difference tae me,' he had said when he gave the field to the village but, as if Selina's good witch had really had a magic wand, things had changed in a twinkling, even, and perhaps especially, for Mr McFadden. 'Well, ye see, I had no counted Timothy,' he said.

That Hallowe'en night, Tim's aunt and uncle had not gone to the pub; they had simply gone. 'Never a thocht for the wee lad,' as Mrs Bridie said indignantly. When the police had taken Tim home, they had found the caravan deserted and locked. The Sergeant had taken him for the night but, 'What'll become of him noo?' asked Mrs Bridie.

Selina knew. While Ma and Mrs Bridie were talking she had got out her bicycle and ridden straight down to the Sergeant's house. She came back in tears. 'I was going to bring Tim here on the back of my bicycle but they won't let me have him. Oh Ma! Tim must come and live with us.'

'Don't be silly,' said Muffet.

'He must.' Selina was frantic. 'He has nowhere else to go, except Sergeant Fraser said he would have to go to a Home! Tim would hate that. Ma, come quickly!'

'We must keep him. Ma, we must.' Tim had been allowed to come, 'Until things are settled,' said Ma, but after two weeks of arguing and visits by 'so many people', to Selina's mystification it still did not seem certain. 'Tim can't go *away*,' she said, appalled.

'It may be he will have to.'

'Why? Why?'

Ma looked worried. 'It's the money,' she said. 'We can hardly make ends meet as it is.'

'Tim doesn't need much,' said Muffet.

'He needs as much as any other child, food and clothes and books and toys and pocket-money.'

'We could give up the ponies,' said Muffet slowly.

'Oh Muffet!' Selina was overwhelmed by the way lofty Muffet could suddenly turn into an ally. 'I don't want Tim to come and live here,' said Muffet, 'but we must be decent.'

'The ponies don't cost much,' said Ma. 'Besides, Great Aunt Emily would want you to keep them.'

'I'll go out to work,' said Selina.

'Where could you work? And who would pay you?' asked Muffet.

'Mrs Bridie would.'

'That would be pretending.'

('Mr McFadden would. He offered to and it wasn't pretending. Mr McFadden never pretends,' said Selina.

He was certainly not pretending now. He came to see Ma. 'It's aboot Tim.'

'Tim?' asked Ma, surprised.

'Aye. Timothy Scobie . . . the boy.'

'What about Tim?'

'Ever since the . . . fuss,' said Mr McFadden with distaste, 'I hae been trying to get some sense int' them. Mrs Russell, I want that bit lad.'

'Want Tim? But . . . for what?' Ma was puzzled. 'For what?'

'For keeps,' said Mr McFadden.

'*Mr McFadden!*' Ma was not surprised now, she was amazed.

'For keeps, but they winnae let me have him. It seems a single man cannae be let to adopt a bairn and mebbe they are richt enough, but . . .' Mr McFadden had taken off his cap when Ma invited him in; now he clenched it in his fist; his eyes blinked.

'But?' Ma prompted him gently.

'If ye would tak him, ma'am,' it came out in a rush, 'I would pay all his expenses.'

'*You!*'

'Ye see,' said Mr McFadden, 'I would wish Timothy to hae a hame, a real hame like this – which I cannae provide – and I wish him to have guid plain schooling. Farming I can teach him and he seems tae tak tae it a'richt, so when I'm gone he shall have Drumlarach and . . . Mrs Russell . . .'

'Yes, Mr McFadden.'

'I'd like it fine if he could take my name and be Timothy McFadden. I . . . I hae come to hae a regard for him,' said Mr McFadden unwillingly, and then he looked at Ma. 'Mrs Russell, please.'

Mr McFadden had not said 'Please' to anyone since he was a grown man.

Hallowe'en came round again.

Selina had never known any year go so quickly and surely no Park was ever made as fast as Menoock Park. 'Because everybody helped,' said Pa.

The men built the walls of local rough stone; the gates were made in the village foundry. Major McBain of the plant-hire firm lent his machines to level the ground and excavate the site for the swimming-pool and, in spring when the lanes and fields were sweet with primroses and violets, the lawns were sown with grass seed. The men dug the flower beds, the women planted them, the children watered and weeded. In May, trees were planted too, blossom trees and rowan. 'A rowan tree means happiness,' said Mrs Bridie. As the swimming pool was made, the weather turned hot and everyone longed to use the pool but, 'Not yet,' said the Committee. 'Not till opening day.' Nor could people sit and look at the roses – there were no benches yet – but the little pavilion was made, 'For when it rains,' said Mrs Bridie and, at the beginning of the autumn term, when the new rowan trees, for all their youngness, showed berries, came a glorious day when the swings, the big see-saw and the slides, all glistening with green and red paint and clean new ropes, arrived for the playground. No work was done in school that afternoon and, at break, rows of small faces looked longingly over the wall that separated the dull old school playground from the Park. 'Can't we just go in and try them?'

'Not yet,' said the Committee.

That autumn, too, the bowling green was made. 'But it will be a while before ony yin can play,' said Mrs Bridie. 'The grass must be cut and raked, cut and raked, until it's velvet. Aye! It will be bonnie,' said Mrs Bridie.

The Park was to be opened on Hallowe'en. ''Twas Hallowe'en that made Mr McFadden change his mind,' said the Committee. There was to be a grand Hallowe'en party, not only for children, for everyone. 'You'll have to dook for apples,' Selina told Pa. Everyone was to bring a lump of coal. 'That's the luckiest thing,' – the coal would be built into the bonfire that stood ready – and champers, sausages and other good things would be brought up to the school hall. The party was to be held after the opening which would be just at dusk. The Provost was to make a speech, there would be a band, and a red ribbon stretched between the Park gates. When the ribbon was cut, the Park would be open, but who was to do the cutting? 'Mr McFadden.' That was unanimous but, 'Not on yer life,' said Mr McFadden.

'But you gave the field.'

'I dinnae hae tae come after it.'

'Then who?'

'Ask Selina Russell. It's her doing,' said Mr McFadden but, when Selina was asked, she quailed. 'I couldn't.'

'I think you could,' said Ma.

'No, please no,' Selina implored. 'Not in front of everyone.' Even the thought appalled her. 'Muffet would do it beautifully.'

Muffet would have liked to – *The Park was declared open by Miss Marguerite Russell* – but, 'It's not me they want,' Muffet had to say. 'It's you.'

'I know what we'll do,' said Ma. 'Let all the children dress up and wear their masks – they always do for Hallowe'en – then no one will know it is Selina.'

'Mr McFadden and Mrs Bridie will know.'

'They won't tell.'

'And Muffet and Elspeth and Susan – all the girls.'

'We won't tell,' promised Muffet.

'And the boys. If I'm a good witch, Stuart and Ian and the other big boys will know.'

'They won't tell. They would be ashamed to.'

It might have seemed to Selina that the number of people who would not tell was the larger part of Menoock. 'But Selina believes things,' as Muffet said; besides, the pink mask made her feel safely hidden and, when Ma asked, 'Will you do it?,' 'If you say so . . .' said Selina.

'I'll be the same old bat,' said Muffet.

'I'll stay a good witch,' said Selina and Tim did not have to steal anyone's nightdress. Ma made him an elf dress with green tights, a green tunic and a red cap with a white feather in it and, 'I'm a n'imp,' said Tim. 'I'm a spunkie.'

Perhaps the best thing of that exciting year had been watching the change in Tim, Timothy McFadden as he was now; his face was brown from the sun and rosy; his legs were no longer like pea-sticks; he was fatter all over, almost sturdy; his eyes did not look as sunken in his face. There were no more bruises, no outsize ragged clothes; Tim had jeans and shorts and jerseys like any boy, 'and shoes with *soles*,' whispered Tim. 'Leather shoes not plimsolls and I got six pairs of socks.' His hair was brushed and cut; his nails were clean, he was clean all over. In the summer he went with the Russells to the seaside and was so overcome that, when he came back, he could not tell Mr McFadden about it; he could only stand by his chair and say, 'I seen the sea,' but it was like a chant.

He went to school that autumn riding his own bicycle – 'A new bicycle, not old,' said Tim in wonder. 'I had a birthday!' He had never had a birthday before. Sometimes, though, Pa dropped him on his way to work and Ma fetched him; Tim, who had walked nearly a mile to school from the caravan, could perfectly well have gone and come on his own, but he loved to be fetched. 'I got a family now. I got a Ma and a Pa,' said Tim. 'I got two Pa's' – his real Pa was Mr McFadden. Tim spent most of his evenings and all his weekends at Drumlarach; when he could not go there, if it were too dark and cold and rainy, sometimes, with Lady and Big Wullie, Mr McFadden would walk down to the Russells – his foot had quite healed now. Big Wullie stayed on the terrace but sometimes Mr McFadden would drink a dram with Pa, sometimes he and Lady had tea with the children which he seemed to like best of all. 'Ye're fine and easy in here,' he would say to them, 'and yer Ma sets a good table,' but, 'Ye mustn't let me be a burden to ye, Mrs Russell,' he said anxiously.

'You're welcome, Mr McFadden, not only to us – it's important for Tim.'

'Aye, Tim,' and Mr McFadden's gaze dwelt on Tim's brushed hair, his clean sturdier body, the brown eyes, so contented now, the way Tim's smiles, not so rare now, had begun to curl up at the corners. 'He's happy.'

'I'm happy from here to here,' Tim could have said, happy from the soles of the shoes he thought so much of to the top of his head.

'*I declare this Park open. I declare this Park open. I declare . . .*'

'That's what you have to say.' Muffet had dinned it into Selina's head. '*I declare this Park open*, loudly and clearly. Then you cut the ribbon. Don't get it the other way round,' said Muffet.

'I don't want to do it,' Selina protested for perhaps the hundredth time.

'Ride there on Haggis and you'll never get there.' Muffet was unsympathetic. 'I'm sure she'll make a muddle,' she told Ma.

Now the whole of Menoock was gathered around the Park gates, each family bringing its good luck lump of coal. The bonfire was ready to be lit, 'and there will be fireworks.' Tim had said that over and over again. The Park itself was floodlit; they could see all the delectable things waiting. Its walls were draped with flags, there were streamers across the street and every small child was to have a balloon. 'Not us, we're too old,' said Muffet, but Selina did not think so. Through the crowd, a lane was roped off, 'For the important people,' said Muffet. 'You ought to be there,' she told Selina. 'Not on your life,' said Selina, copying Mr MᶜFadden. 'What a pity,' said Ma, 'that he won't be there,' but Mr MᶜFadden had gruffly refused to come. The members of the Committee would be in the important place – Pa was among them now – with the Minister, Mr Doherty the headmaster, Doctor Dinwiddie and the Provost wearing his gold chain.

When the Provost had made his speech, praising Great Aunt Emily and Mr McFadden 'for their munificent gifts', he came across and, from the rows of children in their fancy dresses, singled out Selina – He knows me by my pink witch's hat – took her by the hand and led her to the waiting ribbon. A cheer went up with a clapping that buzzed in Selina's ears; the lights seemed to dazzle under her mask; her heart was beating so loudly she thought the Provost would hear it and her legs were trembling. A pair of scissors was put into her hand and the Provost gave her a gentle push towards the ribbon.

This was where she had to say, '*I declare . . .*' but all words had left Selina. 'How queer you are!' Muffet had said. 'You weren't frightened when Mr McFadden was hurt in the field and there was all that blood. Yet you're so frightened of this!' Selina tried, she swallowed, licked her dry lips but no sound came. Tears began to run down her cheeks under the mask. 'Go *on*!' She caught an anguished whisper from Muffet. Selina gathered herself together so that all of her seemed to run up into the point of her hat; she took a firm grip of the scissors. '*Open*,' bellowed Selina and snapped the scissors; the beautiful ribbon, cut in half, fell at her feet. 'Well done,' said the Provost, but Selina was past hearing or understanding and, 'I cut it. I cut it,' she wailed.

The cheers turned to laughing and again the people clapped. 'Aye, you cut it!' 'That's the girl.' 'That's a brave lass. Of course you cut it.' Even the Provost was laughing. It was too much for Selina; she turned and ran.

'Where are you going?' She heard the Provost call.

'Pell-mell. Anywhere, out of here,' Selina would

have said but there was no time to speak. She ran past the people, the faces and the clapping hands, ran, 'as if she were Haggis bolting,' said Muffet. Selina would have run home but she heard a sound, so loud and so insistent that it stopped her. It was a cackling, a loud interested cackling and, Big Wullie, thought Selina.

She stopped so abruptly that she slid, and yes, there at the back of the crowd, behind it and standing apart, she saw the four of them, her own four; Big Wullie; Lady; Tim and Mr McFadden.

'Mr McFadden!' Selina hurled herself at him crying, 'Mr McFadden,' – 'Crying! You were shouting!' Muffet told her afterwards – 'Mr McFadden.'

The crowd heard and, in a moment, Selina's cry was taken up. The people who had faced the Park and the Provost turned the other way. 'McFadden.' 'We want McFadden.' It rolled over Menoock and away to the hills. There had never been such an unanimous chorus. 'We want Angus. We want McFadden.'

Someone – perhaps it was Pa – took Selina away; hands propelled Mr McFadden forward, then he was lifted shoulder high. Tim had the presence of mind to hold Lady by the collar, Big Wullie round the neck, but he shouted with the rest: 'McFadden! McFadden!' Mr McFadden was put down by the Provost who wrung his hand. Mr McFadden was clapped on the shoulder; there was clapping and laughter all around. Then, as the Provost held up his hand, silence fell and, 'Angus, say a few words,' said the Provost.

It was as bad for Mr McFadden as it had been for Selina. He took off his cap, the same old cap they had seen every alternate Friday; the leather of his old tortoise face worked, but no more than Selina had he any words. The cap went round and round in his hands, the people waited, then: 'Thank ye,' said Mr McFadden. That was as strange a word for him as 'please'.

'It's we who should thank you,' began the Provost, but Mr McFadden interrupted.

'Och!' he said testily. Then, 'Is it no time for the party?' he asked.

'But you said you wouldn't come to *anything*,' said Selina.

'It's that wee pest Tim. He wouldnae come withoot me and, of course, I couldnae let him miss it. He's a blackmailer, that Tim,' but, before the first rocket soared into the sky, Mr McFadden had tasted champers. 'At last,' said Selina.

'Have you ever been to a party before?' asked Ma.

'Not in my life.' He said 'in my life', not 'on my life', which again was new to Mr McFadden.

'Are you enjoying it?'

Mr McFadden was not going as far as that. 'It's interesting,' he said.

'We'll not be putting a turf on your chimney this Hallowe'en, Mr McFadden,' Ian Robb sang out.

'Cheeky young devil.' Mr McFadden seemed back at his crankiest but when Stuart called, 'Maybe, though, you'd like us to tie up Selina,' 'I've thocht of it myself, muny times,' answered Mr McFadden. 'Mebbe tonicht though we should let her go free,' and, 'Mr McFadden made a joke!' Ma told Pa.

A little later they began the apple dooking: a tub of water was put in the middle of the floor, apples floated in it, and people, their hands tied behind them, had to kneel and try to bite an apple. Mr McFadden watched Pa and Elspeth, against each other, kneeling each side of the tub; they chased the apples round and round. Elspeth's hair was dripping, her chin was wet; Pa was more skilful but it was difficult to tell which of them was laughing the most. 'Antics!' said Mr McFadden but he sounded wistful. 'I should hae liked that fine when I was a lad.'

'You could dook for an apple now,' suggested Selina and, to her and Ma's and everyone's amazement, Mr McFadden did.

He did not, though, stay long. The party was too noisy and crowded for Mr McFadden and soon he was on his way up the lane to Drumlarach. Lady padded beside him; she had had a good supper, but Big Wullie had had too much. Once the children lost their fear of him, they had given him so many tidbits that he could scarcely waddle; in fact, he was so stuffed and drowsy, so slow, that Mr McFadden had to carry him. 'My! You're a gye weight,' but children or gander, it made no difference now to Mr McFadden; he was accustomed; often, when Tim's legs were tired, he carried him back from the Far Field. 'But he carried me first,' said Selina, jealously.

'He carries me more often than he carries you,' flashed Tim. Mr McFadden did not, of course, let them know it, but he could not help feeling pleased when they quarrelled over him.

On the gateposts at Drumlarach were two turnip lanterns; Mr McFadden had hollowed them and carved them and put them there – he had seldom

enjoyed anything as much. They were still alight as he
came up the lane and their flickering greeted him. 'But
Selina and Tim should hae seen them,' he told Lady
and Big Wullie.

He set the gander in his pen, delivering him up to his wives who crowded round him, cackling and obviously asking endless questions. 'Little clashbags,' said Mr McFadden. Then he and Lady went to the farmhouse but, before going in, he paused at the door.

It was not only the houses where there were children that had set turnip lanterns at their gates that night; it was every house in Menoock and, from Drumlarach doorway, Mr M'Fadden could see them, chains or beads of light – like glowworms, or spunkies, thought Mr M'Fadden. Selina's poem came into his head:

> Listen, listen, listen, listen
> Glisten, glisten, glisten, glisten.

Mr McFadden was listening.

This Hallowe'en there were no small dressed-up figures flitting from house to house, thought Mr McFadden. They were all at the party. He could hear the hum and, faintly, its music. A rocket sped up in the sky; probably the boys had found one left over from the display; it exploded into a shower of red stars that lit up the hills, Drumlarach and the glen. They went out, leaving the quiet mystery of the night, quiet but spunkie-haunted – for me and Tim and Selina, thought Mr McFadden.

Yesterday he had told Selina, 'There's a lady come to Craigieburn Farm, an' she rides. I hear she's a wonder with horses. Mebbe if we took Haggis to her, she might bring back his mouth.'

Selina said nothing.

'If she did, he wouldnae tak' off for the neep field.'

Selina still said nothing.

'Well, don't ye want him cured?'

'No,' said Selina. 'I don't.'

Listen, listen, listen, listen

Mr McFadden stood listening. He looked down at the turnip lanterns. Then, full content, he called Lady and went in and shut the door.

Rumer Godden, novelist, playwright and poet, was born in 1907 in Sussex and spent the early years of her childhood in India. When she was twelve, she and her three sisters were sent to school in England, but later she went back to India and has been going backward and forward ever since, perpetually homesick for one or the other.

Distinguished for the exceptionally wide range of her writing, Miss Godden has achieved great success in the field of children's books. These are about small things – dolls, mice, and little girls, and in such charming and delicate stories as *The Dolls' House*, *Miss Happiness and Miss Flower*, *Little Plum*, *The Story of Holly and Ivy* (all published in Puffins), *The Mousewife*, *Mouse House*, *The Kitchen Madonna* and *Operation Sippacik*, she has established a reputation as one of the leading authors writing today for children. Her translations from the French of Carmen Bernos de Gasztold's enchanting *Prayers from the Ark* appeared in 1963, followed by a further volume, *The Beasts' Choir*, in 1967. Miss Godden now lives in Rye, Sussex, in a house which once belonged to Henry James.

Also in Puffins is *The Diddakoi*, recently televised as *Kizzy*.

If you have enjoyed reading this book and would like to know about others which we publish, why not join the Puffin Club? You will be sent the club magazine, *Puffin Post*, four times a year and a smart badge and membership book. You will also be able to enter all the competitions. For details of cost and an application form, send a stamped addressed envelope to:

The Puffin Club Dept A
Penguin Books Limited
Bath Road
Harmondsworth
Middlesex

and if you live in Australia, please write to:

The Australian Puffin Club
Penguin Books Australia Limited
P.O. Box 257
Ringwood
Victoria 3134